Cowboy Falling Hard

Coming Home to North Dakota, Volume 8

Jessie Gussman

Published by Jessie Gussman, 2022.

This is a work of fiction. Similarities to real people, places, or events are entirely coincidental.

COWBOY FALLING HARD

First edition. September 21, 2022.

Copyright © 2022 Jessie Gussman.

Written by Jessie Gussman.

Cover art by Julia Gussman[1]
Editing by Heather Hayden[2]
Narration by Jay Dyess[3]
Author Services by CE Author Assistant[4]

LISTEN TO THE UNABRIDGED audio performed by Jay Dyess HERE[5] on the Say with Jay channel on YouTube. Hear many of Jessie's other books performed by Jay for FREE on Say with Jay.

CLICK HERE[6] if you'd like to subscribe to my newsletter and find out why people say, "Jessie's is the only newsletter I open and read" and "You make my day brighter. Love, love, love reading your newsletters. I don't know where you find time to write books. You are so busy living life. A true blessing." and "I know from now on that I can't be drinking my morning coffee while reading your newsletter – I laughed so hard I sprayed it out all over the table!"

---

1. https://www.sweetlibertydesigns.com/

2. https://hhaydeneditor.com/

3. https://www.facebook.com/SayWithJay

4. http://www.ceauthorassistant.com/

5. https://www.youtube.com/c/SaywithJay/videos

6. https://BookHip.com/FASFD

Chapter 1

Let your differences be your strengths. We've been married forty years and figured this out early on. Hubs is big picture I do the detailed things. It has worked for us. Also don't sweat the small stuff. Just this week we were nit picking each other and I stopped and said we don't do this to each other. We were able to stop the behavior. - Pam from the Bay Area CA

"THIS IS MY FRIEND DWIGHT Eckenrode, and he would like to use your services."

Dwight, standing in the churchyard in Sweet Water, North Dakota, didn't usually shrink away from attention.

He was one of the best baseball players in the country, and he was used to cameras and crowds and adulation.

What he was not used to was having his best friend in the world, Bryce Shaker, introduce him in such a way to a group of old ladies sitting at a picnic table beside a little country church and having all of their eyes widen and look at him like they were trying to figure out what was wrong with him that he would need the services of matchmakers.

The lady with blue hair spoke. "Dwight would like a quilt?" Her voice sounded incredulous.

Dwight had the oddest urge to laugh hysterically. Probably nerves.

"No." Bryce, the cracker head, smirked.

Dwight wouldn't mind wiping the smirk from his face. This was not something he wanted to joke about.

He had been trying for eighteen months to catch the eye of Orchid Baldwin. Her family owned the auction house in Sweet Water, and in the last eighteen months, Dwight had found every excuse he could to travel from Houston, where he played for the professional baseball team there, to North Dakota, on the pretense of visiting his friend. He would bet he'd gone to more auctions than most people who actually lived in North Dakota, but Orchid never seemed to notice him.

"Not your quilting services, although we appreciate them," Bryce said, with another side smirk. "But your matchmaking services."

"Oh, we're not for hire, are we, Charlene?" a lady sitting beside the blue-haired lady said.

"We might be, Teresa. Hear them out." The blue-haired lady said the words slyly, like she already knew what he was going to say.

Despite how serious he felt about the situation, Dwight was tempted to smile. The blue-haired lady was his kind of girl. Even if she was thirty years older than he was.

Dwight looked around, not wanting to be overheard by anyone else in the churchyard. It was full, with people milling about, but no one was paying any attention to them.

"I heard you're quite good at what you do." A little compliment for the ladies wouldn't hurt, he was sure. "I've been trying to catch the eye of a girl here in town for a long time, and I haven't been successful. Bryce recommended I hire you."

"I'm not comfortable being for hire," Teresa insisted.

The other ladies were shaking their heads as well, but Charlene's expression was considering.

"Are you moving to Sweet Water?"

Bryce had told him to make sure he told them that he was. But he couldn't say something that wasn't true. People did it all the time, but lying was something he would never be comfortable with.

He hesitated for a moment.

Charlene shook her head. "We don't match our hometown girls with men who are going to move them away." She lifted her shoulder. "Sorry."

"I only hesitated because I wanted to make sure I told you the truth. I have one year left on my contract that keeps me in Houston, but I'm thinking about retiring at the end of the season."

He might be one of the best ballplayers in the country, but baseball wasn't as fulfilling to him as it used to be. He was restless. Wanted more of...something. Felt like his life was empty, a big void that needed to be filled.

"Come back when you're sure of it." Charlene waved a hand, dismissing him again.

"I promise if you help me, I won't move anyone away from Sweet Water."

"His word is good. I'll vouch for him."

Dwight wanted to hug his friend. He felt like his word was good, but to have his friend jump in without him asking and vouch for him made his chest swell. It pushed away some of the emptiness he'd just been thinking about and made him think that maybe that's what he needed. Someone who believed in him. A town full of people who had each other's backs. He'd been in Sweet Water long enough to know that's what they were.

He wanted to be a part of that.

He wanted his family to be a part of that.

"Which girl?" Charlene asked, her eyes looking sharp and intelligent.

"Orchid Baldwin." He glanced around again, not wanting word to get out that he was hiring the matchmakers or attempting to. He figured the whole town already knew he was interested in Orchid. He figured they also already knew that she wasn't the slightest bit interested in him.

It was a bit of a blow for his pride. After all, in the world he inhabited, he didn't have any trouble getting dates.

Not until he came to Sweet Water.

"You've asked Orchid out before, haven't you?" Charlene said, her finger tapping her chin. The other ladies leaned in, as though they wanted to catch every word. He didn't know how they made their plans or did what they did, but he knew that Bryce credited them with getting him and his fiancée, Peyton, together. And they'd done it in such a way that Bryce hadn't realized what they were doing.

After all, if a man felt pushed in one direction, he almost always felt the need to push back, even if he was cutting off his nose to spite his face.

"I have. Multiple times. She said no every time." He didn't believe in being a show-off, exactly. But he had tried to impress upon her that he was successful, athletic—he hadn't been above flashing a few muscles or his killer dimple. He let her know that he knew how to show her a good time and would take her out of this slow-as-molasses, cowpoke town. As much as he admired Sweet Water and the people in it, he figured it had to get boring. All Orchid ever seemed to do was work and help people.

He could afford to do things that would make her smile. Travel. Have people waiting on them hand and foot and enjoy the easy life.

Nothing he'd said or done had made any kind of impression on her.

"That says to me that she's probably not interested," Charlene said, the expression on her face not changing.

Dwight wasn't sure what to say about that. He didn't feel like he had stalked her. Asking her out five times in twelve months or so wasn't really nagging. Was it?

He always took no for an answer, without trying to push her into anything.

He still tried to strike up conversations with her, talking about baseball, workouts, Houston, and traveling, talking about some of the places he'd been, like his vacation on the Mediterranean and sightseeing in Paris.

He left out the fact that he'd been with a couple of his exes during those trips. He wasn't a complete idiot. He didn't talk about the women he'd dated with the woman he wanted to be with. Since he'd met Orchid, he hadn't wanted to be with anyone else, anyway.

"You're saying I should give up?" He finally spoke when Charlene seemed like she wasn't inclined to.

"Give up or change your strategy."

"That's why I'm coming to you."

Charlene nodded, matter-of-factly, like she'd already figured that out but just wanted to make sure.

"Do you think you'll take me on?" he felt compelled to ask.

"I think we're going to need to talk about it and discuss it amongst ourselves." Charlene looked around the group of ladies, who didn't exactly look eager to take on a non-native.

That was the one thing he didn't like about small towns. They were very closed off to any kind of change, and that included new people in town.

Cities didn't have that kind of problem. They accepted everyone with open arms, then promptly forgot about them.

He supposed it was better to be a little standoffish at first, and then when they accepted someone, they made a commitment for life.

That's the way a small town was.

Their standoffishness with strangers was a self-preservation thing, because if too many people from different backgrounds flooded in, the town no longer was a safe, welcoming haven, but the very fabric of the town would be changed and most likely not for the better. There were reasons people left the big cities.

He understood all of that and didn't consider it wrong. If someone wanted to protect their heritage, if a town wanted to keep their safe borders, he couldn't fault them.

Even if that meant he had to earn his spot here.

Charlene's eyes narrowed even more, if that were possible. "I think it's a valid question for me to ask you what you see in Orchid?"

As he figured, Charlene was not surprised to find out exactly who he had been talking about.

There was so much that attracted him to Orchid. How did he explain it? He looked around, then lowered his voice.

"She has integrity. She works hard. She doesn't lose her temper or get irritated. Kids love her, and she always takes time for them. She helps her family and seems to have good relationships with all of them. I definitely think she would be someone who would be easy to get along with and would put others first. She's different than every other girl I know. Better."

That wasn't everything. But he just couldn't put his finger on why she was so compelling to him. There was some kind of...glow about her.

Not that she was happy all the time, but that she just seemed to walk in peace. There was a calmness, and while she didn't strike him as an overly confident person, she seemed to know what she wanted. Although, he'd almost say she was the kind of person who was in her head a lot and didn't allow the things that happened around her to upset her.

It contrasted with his more aggressive personality. He'd gotten his temper mostly under control from his younger days, but he definitely didn't have calmness or peace. He had a drive to be the best, do his best, and go after what he wanted. That was probably why he hadn't been scared off when Orchid had turned him down. Probably why he was standing here now, in front of the notorious matchmakers, even though the possibility of him being humiliated was high.

Because the possibility of getting what he wanted was just as good.

"I think there might be some things you need to learn," Charlene said, her lips pursed.

Dwight refused to take her words as an insult. "I'm not perfect. I do want to be a better man."

Charlene nodded, like he'd said the right thing. She pressed her lips together and took several deep breaths through her nose. "I'll tell you what," she finally said. "When you close on the house you buy in Sweet Water, you let me know."

He glanced at Bryce, who shrugged his shoulders just a bit. Like he didn't really know what to make of that. As far as Dwight knew, and all he knew was what Bryce had told him, the Piece Makers had never accepted an outside offer of matchmaking.

If they accepted him, he'd be the first.

"I have already been looking. I'll talk to my real estate agent this afternoon." If he could, he'd be putting an offer on a house by Monday night.

"You do that." Charlene smiled, but he felt like it was a smile that didn't quite reach her eyes, like she didn't quite trust him.

"Thanks for your time, ladies. Can I get you anything?" Bryce said, and Dwight wished that he would have thought to offer.

But the ladies shook their heads, and he and Bryce walked away.

They were halfway back to where Peyton sat with Bryce's daughter, Kendrick, and her own son, Owen, out of earshot of the ladies, when Bryce said, "I think that went pretty well. I hoped that they would take you right away, but they seem to be thinking about it, and I do think they're your best bet."

It felt like they were his only bet, but he hadn't gotten to be successful in his baseball career by taking no for an answer.

"I'm happy to wait if there's even a small chance. I've already waited this long, I can keep waiting."

Just because he was waiting didn't mean he wouldn't jump on an opportunity if it presented itself. He had every intention of doing that. If God opened the door, he wouldn't hesitate to run through it.

Chapter 2

Communication. - Linda Rorex; USA

"HE'S HERE TODAY. AND staring at you." Daphne Rolland leaned close to Orchid's ear, probably speaking low so her daughter, Powell, wouldn't hear.

Orchid had been babysitting Powell a good bit since Daphne's mother had had a knee replacement. It had gotten infected, and she was probably going to have to have it replaced again. She'd been off it for several months, and if they couldn't get the new infection under control, she would be off of it for several more.

"I know. I saw him." She tried to keep disinterest in her voice as she pursed her lips deliberately.

She had to admit the baseball player's interest was flattering. And in a deeper part of her heart, away from prying eyes, she could admit there was something about him that made her eyes want to wander over and latch onto him.

It wasn't because he was handsome, and it wasn't because he was a famous baseball player. He had something else, something she couldn't explain. But she figured it was probably something that appealed to the fleshly part of her, since he wasn't the kind of man she wanted to end up with.

"I bet he'll ask you out again. It's been at least a month since the last time," her twin sister, Lavender, said with a smirk, casting a furtive glance at Powell, who had knelt down and was petting a mama cat.

"I hope not. I feel bad telling him no all the time. You'd think he'd get the hint."

"You have to admire a man who is determined," Daphne said, with a little bit of wistfulness in her voice.

It made Orchid think of Powell and who her father might be. Daphne had never said, and Orchid hated to pry. Just the fact that Powell didn't know made her think that there was some secret Daphne was hiding.

"I think you don't want him to take the hint." Her twin sister, who knew her better than anyone else in the world, lifted her brows and gave her a knowing look.

When they had a rare break, Orchid didn't usually wish the auction would hurry up and get started again, but they were finished with the calves and removing some animals around the back. Lavender and she were helping to load the animals that were sold, and right now, they were just waiting.

She didn't want to have to answer her sister, though, so she was tempted to step out and go see if the people in the back needed help.

But that was cowardly, and cowardly was not a word she wanted to use to describe herself.

"I think there's probably something in every woman that wants to be chased the way he seems to be chasing me." And that was true. She could admit that she was flattered. "But..."

"Why don't you say yes?" Daphne asked, truly perplexed. She didn't usually make it to the auction, hadn't in a long time, since her dad had been killed in a farming accident and she and her mom had been alone on the farm, and especially since her mom's knee replacement.

In fact, Orchid thought this might be only the first or second time she'd seen Dwight.

"He might be a nice person, but he's always bragging. Not, not exactly bragging, but he just talks about things that take a lot of money, like fancy restaurants and trips, which I assume he probably took with other women, and I'm sure he knows that I know that, so it's kind of like he's not only bragging about where he's been but that he's been there with other women. Maybe he doesn't mean to, but it doesn't impress me. It's a turnoff."

"Yeah. That's yucky."

"I don't really think he means it to be, but he just doesn't realize how it's coming across."

"I think he's trying to impress her, and he doesn't know how to do it. Maybe those kinds of things impress the girls he's used to being around." Lavender had a certain amount of sense in her words.

And Orchid had admitted that to her before. She looked at Daphne. "Lavender might be right, but that doesn't change the fact that those are the things he thinks would impress me, which means that he doesn't know me."

"But he wants to get to know you! How can he if you won't talk to him?"

Orchid's eyes slid toward the stands. Dwight sat with Boone and Roxie Stryker and some of their kids. She didn't even know that he knew Boone and Roxie. Of course, as much as he'd been hanging around Sweet Water, it made sense that he would have met the owners of the ranch that gave Sweet Water its name.

They were engaged in conversation, but as she watched, Dwight's eyes scanned the area where she was standing, almost as though he knew she was there, and they landed on her.

Normally she would be embarrassed at being caught staring, but...she didn't jerk her eyes away like she was tempted to do.

Instead, she gazed steadily back at him.

He didn't seemed embarrassed that he'd been caught looking for her, or maybe he didn't think of it like that.

Whatever it was, they stared at each other across the arena and the heads of people and the walkway that separated them.

Folks were chatting, and gradually Orchid realized Lavender and Daphne were saying something else, but she didn't hear. Wasn't paying attention to them.

There was something compelling about him.

She already admitted that much to herself, but even while she knew it, she also knew he wasn't the kind of man she was interested in. Not even a little.

"Did you hear me, Orchid?" Daphne asked, her voice finally cutting through Orchid's brain haze.

Reluctantly, Orchid pulled her eyes away. Really, she should never have allowed herself to meet his gaze. He'd probably be down here later, trying to ask her out again.

Why not say yes?

Because he wasn't the kind of man she wanted to be with. She wasn't going to date just for the fun of it. She was not wasting her time on someone she would never have a future with. She didn't want to take the risk of falling for someone who was so completely wrong for her.

"No. I'm sorry I didn't. What did you say?" she asked, noticing that they were bringing the last of the hogs into the pen and were getting ready to start the auction again.

"I heard he was talking to the Piece Makers Sunday after church." Daphne lifted her brows and gave Orchid a knowing look. "I wonder what he could have been saying to them? Wink wink."

"Maybe he was offering to bring them drinks. Or maybe they were talking about the weather. That seems to be what everybody talks about at church socials." Farmers couldn't get enough of talking about the weather, what it had done, what it was doing, what it was going to do that afternoon, that evening, overnight, and for the rest of their lives.

Not that she blamed them, since their livelihood depended on what the weather did, but she did get a little tired of rehashing it over and over. She wanted to talk about interesting things, not things she couldn't do anything about.

Or maybe she was just restless and wanted something to complain about.

"That's not why people talk to the Piece Makers." Daphne crossed her arms over her chest and tapped her foot. "And you know it."

Orchid couldn't disagree.

"I'd better go." Daphne looked down at Powell who was still squatting down, petting the kittens. "It's time to go, honey. I'm sure we can come back and see the kitties again sometime."

"Thanks for coming over and chatting with us," Orchid said, and Lavender chimed in her agreement.

Daphne walked away, and Lavender closed the distance between them, putting her arm around Orchid.

"You know, sometimes people do pretty strange things to catch people's attention. But everything I've been hearing around town says that he's an alright guy."

"I haven't heard anything bad about him, either. But that doesn't mean I want to date him."

"That's what dating is for. To decide whether you like him or not."

"But I don't want to date someone that I know I won't be interested in, even if I do decide I like him. That's the problem. I don't want to like him and let my feelings dictate my actions. I want to make deliberate choices."

Maybe that was boring. People had made fun of her over the years for thinking too much, being in her head, being quiet and serious and deliberate in what she did.

But Lavender understood. The arm around her tightened.

"That is so like you. But maybe sometimes your vision is a little narrow."

Orchid looked at the ground. She knew that to be true. Sometimes she got an idea in her head, and she couldn't shake it. She latched on and couldn't be persuaded otherwise.

Was that what this was?

It couldn't be. She was sure that Dwight was not right for her.

"You don't want to miss out on what you're supposed to do because you refused to open your eyes to the possibilities."

She looked at her sister, knowing she would never give her advice that she thought might hurt her or wouldn't be best for her.

"This is one of those times where I'm not seeing things because I'm so sure that what I think I know is all there is to know?"

Lavender shook her head. "I don't know. But I do know when a man chases a girl the way Dwight has chased you, the way he has allowed you to put him off but not be dissuaded, the way he's admired you, no matter how much you didn't encourage him, if he truly is that dedicated to you, I don't think you could go wrong with him, since he seems to be a man of character and integrity."

Lavender looked across the arena as the first hog of the night stepped on the scale. In a softer voice, she said, "I wish there was some man who admired me like that. It has to make you feel like you're worth something."

"You're worth something!" Orchid said, concern for her sister making her forget about the auction, and the people around, and the man across the arena, who was looking at her again.

"I know. I know my worth is in Christ, but I don't think it's wrong for us to desire the love and affection of a man. Isn't that a desire God gave us?"

"Yeah. I'm sure it is. It's just sad that it's something we seem to need, because you don't. You don't need a man in order to make you feel worthy."

"I know. I didn't mean it that way, I just meant it's an inborn desire to have a mate. And to have one who appreciates you and loves you for who you are."

"And the ability to give that back to him."

"Of course. Marriage is a two-way street, not something that is supposed to benefit one party exclusively."

The auctioneer pounded his gavel on his little stand and called out, "Sold!"

Orchid and Lavender split apart, going to their respective places in order to move the hog out of the arena and into the area where the buyer would eventually back in and load it.

As she worked the rest of the evening, Orchid prayed silently, asking the Lord for wisdom. He promised to give liberally to anyone who asked, and she needed it. She didn't want to make a mistake, not in choosing a life's partner, and end up divorced with a broken home. Or to be married for the rest of her life but miserable. Lonely and alone.

She wanted to make a good decision and marry the man God wanted for her. She needed wisdom to figure out who that was.

By the end of the evening, she had decided to say yes when Dwight came down and asked her on a date, which was usually around ten or so.

After she'd made that decision, she pushed him out of her head, and she and Lavender got busy until the auction was over. There was a constant stream of people loading their animals and leaving.

Usually their brother, Coleman, and sometimes his wife, Sadie, gave them a hand.

But they were both out of town at a horse show, and so Lavender and she would be closing things up tonight.

She had to laugh at herself when Dwight didn't show up.

After ten, she found herself looking for him, but his place in the bleachers was empty. Still, he didn't show up where she was, and she decided it was just as well. Maybe she shouldn't have been so arrogant and sure that he would continue chasing her.

"I bought two Herefords and a black Angus steer," Mr. Reynolds said as he handed her the receipt he'd gotten from the office when he paid for his animals.

She looked at it, checking out the numbers, looking over the pens.

As she did so, she could see a long line of farm trucks, headlights off, parking lights glowing, sitting off to the side. They were going to be working until well after midnight.

"You have your trailer in chute three?" she asked.

"Yeah. And I can give you a hand. Just tell me where to stand."

She placed him by a gate and told him to close it when she had the animals through. Then she walked down the aisle until she got to the pen were his three feeders stood.

They were in a pen with two other cows and a two-year-old bull. She hadn't realized they were penned with additional animals and would need Lavender's help for this, since the bull and cows needed to stay.

Glancing around, she saw her sister all the way down at the other end of the aisle, at gate one, working with a farmer and his new herd of goats.

"Can I give you a hand?"

She whirled, not recognizing Dwight's voice at first.

"Sorry. I didn't mean to scare you."

"You didn't. Not really. I just wasn't expecting anyone to talk to me."

Her eyes met his, and she was reminded of the look they'd shared across the arena.

Maybe he was thinking of that too because he didn't answer her, just held her gaze.

In her experience, he was arrogant, a little cocky even, but always with a ready smile.

Tonight, just now, he wasn't smiling.

Mr. Reynolds was waiting on her, so she didn't linger. Instead, she said, "If you would help me, that would be wonderful."

"You're going to have to tell me what to do."

He seemed willing to listen, which surprised her, because from the few times she'd talked to him, she thought of him as arrogant. She appreciated his humble attitude.

"I need the two red white-faced feeders and the black Angus." She pointed to the three steers. "I'll go in and get them, you stand by the gate and don't let any of the other three out."

"Got it."

She thought about telling him to watch the two-year-old bull, but usually young bulls weren't a problem. She didn't want to take the time to explain something that really didn't need to be said since Dwight would be fine behind the gate if the bull decided to do something unusual.

Moving into the pen, she kept her eye on it, just in case, as she went to get the Angus which was closest to the gate.

She was able to separate him from the others easily, and as she moved him toward the gate, she said, "Open it now!"

He moved immediately, and the Angus went out without any trouble, going down the aisle in the direction she wanted.

"Close it again until I'm ready," she said, and he obeyed immediately.

She moved to get closer to the Herefords, but the entire group moved along with them, and she figured she'd let them walk by the gate and try to separate them out as they came around again.

But Dwight must have thought he could open the gate fast enough, or maybe he thought she just forgot to tell him to open it.

Whatever it was, he opened the gate as the group went by, and as cattle often do, they all charged out the opening, eager to be out of the pen and away from the person who was walking among them.

"Uh, oops," he said, trying to shut the gate, but too late.

"It's okay. It happens to people who've been doing it for years."

"I just saw the red ones going by and thought I could catch them."

"You might have been able to. Once in a while, that'll work. Most of the time, it doesn't."

"Which was probably why you didn't tell me to open the gate."

She looked at him, smiling.

"Sorry. What now?"

She had made it to the edge and let herself out of the gate, latching it behind her.

"Lavender is down at the end. I'll tell her what I want, and we'll separate them out. Maybe whoever bought the other three will be there, and we can load those too. And if not, we'll stick them in an empty pen. Thanks for your help."

"I'll come down and give you hand."

She wasn't expecting that. She glanced at him. He wore a T-shirt, jeans, and boots. Nothing fancy.

Sometimes having someone work with cattle who didn't know what they were doing was worse than doing it by oneself, but in her years of working at the sale barn, she'd spent a lot of time wishing they had more help, and as a general rule, they never turned an offer down.

"Okay. Come on down, and I'll give you instructions when we get there."

She wasn't even tempted to remind him to just do what she said. She figured he'd remember, since it was obvious he was embarrassed he'd let all the animals out.

She was right in her assumption.

While Dwight obviously had no clue how to herd animals, he listened immediately to anything he was told to do and did it to the best of his ability. Although, his ability wasn't always enough to keep animals from escaping or to get them to go where they wanted them to, it was obvious he was trying.

She ignored the look Lavender gave her when they first started working together, and she also ignored the odd feeling in her chest as she watched him, mistakes and all. She might have been able to chalk it up to someone giving them a hand, like often happened when they were shorthanded.

But it felt like more than that. Although she couldn't explain in what way.

As they loaded the last cow onto a trailer and said good night to the last farmer Lavender came over.

"Mom needs to drive out to the Heinisch farm and leave our trailer there so they can load their cows in the morning. She was going to leave the truck, rather than trying to unhook the trailer in the dark. She wanted me to go pick her up. Can you close things up here?"

"Of course," Orchid said, knowing that Lavender wasn't really asking her if she could do it, she was asking if she would, and she was expecting that Orchid would not turn her down.

Of course not. It was her job.

But as Lavender walked away, Orchid's eyes fell on Dwight, who stood with one foot on the second rail of the gate, his forearm resting on the top, his posture relaxed, like this wasn't his first time helping, and he was totally at ease.

She took half a second to admire the way he looked. Not necessarily the strength in his forearms, the way his T-shirt pulled across his shoulders, or even the long, jean-clad legs and boots.

It was more the way he just seemed so comfortable in his own skin. Or maybe it was the way he was looking at her. No one ever looked at her like that before.

Too bad when she talked to him, he only ever seemed to talk about himself. Or to be showing off. Even tonight as they had worked, while he had taken every order and had done his best, she always felt like he was putting a little extra movement into everything he did, trying to catch her eye or impress her. It was almost like he was bragging with his actions.

It was a negative way to look at someone, and she tried not to think about it. It was probably her imagination.

"Thanks so much for helping this evening."

"I enjoyed it. I've always liked things that challenge me physically, and this does."

"Yeah, there's a lot of physical work involved. But once you figure out what animals typically do, it makes it a lot easier."

"That's a lot like baseball," he said, and he launched into a description of how baseball was a mind game and how he'd figured that out.

He followed her around while she turned out the lights and closed doors and left the office, and by the time they were out in the parking lot, she hadn't said much more than, "okay," or "really?"

He finally stopped as they stood beside her car.

"Thanks again for your help."

Again, she tried to push away the feeling that he had been saying everything he was about baseball to impress her. That he wanted her to know how knowledgeable he was. Or something.

It wasn't that she wasn't interested in what he was saying, it was just... She wasn't sure.

"I was hoping you might go out with me on Friday night."

She didn't laugh, but she was tempted to. At the beginning of the night, she had expected this, but she'd forgotten, and he caught her off guard.

"No" was on the tip of her tongue, and then she remembered she had decided she was going to say yes. To give him a chance. Maybe, once he got more comfortable with her, he wouldn't feel like he needed to try to impress her. If that was what he was doing.

Beyond that bluster, or whatever it was, she felt like he had a good heart. And Lavender had said he was a man of character. That was the most important thing.

"I can't do it Friday night. I'm helping Daphne with her daughter."

His eyebrows shot up to the middle of his forehead. Again, she was tempted to laugh, but she didn't. She hadn't meant to shock him. Then, she wasn't sure where the words came from, but she said, "Maybe a different night?"

"Thursday?" he suggested immediately.

"Okay." The word was out of her mouth before she realized what she was even saying.

She'd just agreed to go out on a date with Dwight. After turning him down at least six or seven times, she'd actually said yes. He looked like he was about as surprised as she was.

"Seven okay?"

She nodded, still unable to believe that she had said yes. Was she making a big mistake?

He'd done a lot of talking about himself and been what she considered a show-off. But she had a feeling maybe her friends were right. Maybe he was just trying to catch her eye.

To her surprise, he reached around and opened her car door. She hadn't been expecting such a gallant gesture. It took her a moment before she smiled and said, "Thank you," as she got in.

Maybe their date would turn out better than either one of them thought.

Chapter 3

Continuing to learn and grow together. - Kimberly, Harbour, CA

"SHE SAID YES."

Dwight could hardly contain his excitement. The feeling that he wanted to dance around the parking lot. He hadn't even pulled out before he called his best friend, Bryce Shaker. Knowing Bryce would celebrate with him. Bryce knew about every rejection, and Dwight knew Bryce was pulling for him. Even if the Piece Makers weren't.

"Wow, how did you get her to do that?" Bryce said, not needing to ask who in the world he was talking about. Like a good friend, he knew.

"I helped with the auction and chatted with her in the parking lot. When I asked, she said yes."

He did not usually call his buddies and talk about girls, but Orchid was special.

With his phone on speaker, he pulled out of the auction, going in the opposite direction that Orchid had. Some part of him had wanted to follow her, to make sure she got home okay. Not in a stalker kind of way, but in a way that he was just concerned about her and wanted to protect her. A perfectly natural thing for him to do.

"Maybe you won't need the Piece Makers, then." Bryce's calm voice came over the line, saying exactly what Dwight had been thinking.

"Maybe I won't." He grinned a little to himself, not necessarily at the idea of outsmarting, so to speak, the Piece Makers.

More because his persistence had paid off. Now that he'd gotten what he wanted, he felt the heavy weight of wanting to impress her. Making her see that she was getting something good by being with him. He wanted to do everything perfectly.

"I had two houses I was going to make offers on, but they both got sold out from under me when I had my realtor check on them. I guess it's not as imperative now, if I don't need the Piece Makers, but I really did want to move to Sweet Water. Do you have any insider information on someone who might be selling?"

Bryce chuckled a little, but then he said, "No. But I haven't been paying attention. I'll check around, make a few calls, and see what I can find. And Peyton has a lot of good contacts at the bakeshop. I'll ask her to keep an ear out too."

"Thanks." Dwight tapped the steering wheel. He had been planning on finding a home in Sweet Water, but he'd been staying with Bryce whenever he was in town. And hadn't been in a rush, since Bryce's house was more than big enough, and Bryce had told him he could stay as long as he wanted to.

Now that Bryce was getting married and would have two children and a wife with him, maybe it would be slightly more crowded, but Bryce hadn't urged him to leave in any way.

Still, he felt a little like the odd man out when he was with them now. Not to mention, seeing them together just brought home the fact that he was alone.

By choice, he reminded himself. After all, there were plenty of women in Houston who would have been with him in a heartbeat. But he suspected that was mostly for his money. He wanted a woman who was going to care about him as a man, as a person, and not see dollar signs and prestige when she looked at him.

Guilt did a slow loop around his stomach since he knew his actions had been the very opposite of what he actually wanted. Why would he talk about all of his accomplishments in baseball when he was with Orchid, if he didn't want her to see that but wanted her to see him?

That night, it was difficult for him to go to sleep, because he was trying to figure out where he should take her.

And trying to go over everything in his mind to make sure his date with Orchid would be perfect.

On Thursday, he was early as he pulled into her drive. Five minutes early.

But she was ready and came down the steps as he pulled in. His hands were sweating as he opened his door and got out. She wore jeans and some kind of white flowing top, along with cowgirl boots.

At the auction, her hair was always up in a ponytail, and he wasn't sure if he'd ever seen it down, but tonight, blonde waves flowed around her shoulders. He liked it.

His mouth felt dry, and he tried to clear his throat so his voice came out in the right octave. He was almost successful.

"You look nice." Nice wasn't exactly the word he wanted to use, but he didn't want to overwhelm her. "I have a fun evening planned," he said. Honestly though, as she looked up at him, smiling a little, he couldn't remember any of the things he had wanted to do.

Thankfully, he could at least remember he had wanted to open her door. So he walked around the car and did that. He had wanted to greet her with a hug, but that felt a little bit too much. Again, he didn't want to scare her away.

In the car on the way to Rockerton, he told her stories about his baseball days, making sure she knew he was ready to move to North Dakota. He didn't want her thinking that if she was with him, she'd have to move to Texas.

The bar he'd decided to take her to was packed, even for Thursday night. The online reviews he'd read must have been accurate. Good food, good dancing, good music.

He thought the night went well, even if Orchid was a little quiet. That was her personality after all. And he could talk for both of them. It gave him an opportunity to put his best foot forward and show her all the reasons she would be better off with him.

He'd been to his share of bars, and while it wasn't his favorite place to spend an evening, it was where all of his friends had a good time, and it was where he figured he had the best odds of impressing Orchid.

He sang karaoke, and he wasn't bad. In fact, in the competition they were having that evening, he came in second. The competitive part of his nature wanted first place, but considering there were twenty or more competitors, he wasn't upset.

He was a decent dancer and knew his way around not just the dance floor but the food and the music and the people. It all felt familiar to him, if not exceptionally fun. But he'd do whatever he needed to do to impress Orchid.

And she seemed like she was having a good time.

They finally left the bar, and he felt satisfied he'd done a good job of getting her off the farm, away from the auction barn and all the work she was always doing, and showing her a good time.

He wasn't sure what he talked about on the way home, just filled the silence with words. Wanting to keep the good vibes going.

He was pretty pleased with himself when he pulled into her drive and turned to look at her. If she asked him in, he would go. He wanted to meet her family; although he'd seen all of them at the auction barn at some point, he wanted to meet them. He felt like he could impress them as well.

She didn't say anything as they pulled to a stop, reaching for her door handle.

"Hold on. I'll get it." He didn't always get the door for his dates, but Orchid had seemed like she was surprised and pleased when he had opened it for her to get in.

So he took a chance.

Her hand dropped, and so he jumped out and ran around.

Opening the door, he offered her his hand, but she must not have seen it, because she got out without taking it.

"Thank you for this evening," she said as she stopped in front of his car.

"You're welcome. I had a great time."

She nodded but didn't say anything. She probably didn't know how to put into words how much she enjoyed it.

"I'd love to do it again. Can I call you tomorrow?" He wanted her phone number. He should have gotten it earlier.

He had his hand reaching into his back pocket before he realized she was shaking her head.

"Thanks, but...I don't think so."

His hand froze and his mouth hung open, but he seemed unable to close it.

"You didn't have a good time?" That couldn't be it. It had to be him. "You don't like me?"

That seemed like such a lame thing to say, and he hated the words as they came out of his mouth, but he said them anyway.

He should have kept his mouth shut, turned, and walked away. But...he'd tried so hard. How could he have not been successful?

Not to mention, he liked her. Really liked her. More than he'd ever liked any girl he dated before.

"I like you," she said, and she didn't hesitate. Her eyes, looking into his, were sincere. He didn't doubt that.

"Can I ask what the issue is?"

He didn't want to. But at the same time, he really did. He wanted to know where he failed. Because he didn't see it.

But she shook her head.

"I just...don't think we have a lot in common." She smiled gently up at him. "There's nothing wrong with you. It's me."

Cliché.

Maybe there was usually some truth to clichés. That's why they were clichés, but he hated that one. Hated hearing it come out of her mouth. It made it seem like there was nothing he could do.

But he didn't want to stand here and keep her. Didn't want to draw the evening out if she hadn't enjoyed herself.

Feeling more dejected than he could ever remember feeling, even three years ago when they'd lost the pennant, he nodded his head. "I'm sorry. I had a great time, so...thank you. And I'm sorry you didn't."

"You're a great person. I hope you find someone who really appreciates you."

Chapter 4

Realizing and showing your partner how important they are to you. - Teresa, California

DWIGHT WANTED TO ASK Orchid why she couldn't appreciate him, but even more than that, he just wanted to leave.

"Let me walk you to your door." The night was chilly, the wind even colder, and there were clouds skittering across the sky, blocking out the moon, casting shadows, making the deep night even blacker.

She nodded, and they walked up the walk side by side. They just said goodbye at the door and nothing else.

He didn't want to go to Bryce's house. He hardly thought Bryce would be waiting up to talk to him, but just in case, he didn't want to take that chance. He didn't feel like talking.

So he drove the short distance back into Sweet Water and parked along the street.

Leaving the key in his truck, he got out, unsure of what he was doing. All the shops were dark. There were no lights in any of the windows and no movement on the sidewalk or streets. Not even a TV blinked giving a sign that there might be human life awake at this hour.

Sweet Water might as well be a ghost town, and it was barely midnight.

Lord? What did I do wrong?

He hadn't always been a praying man. In his younger days, he'd been pretty cocky and sure of himself, feeling like his success was due to everything he had done rather than something he had faith in. And it was certainly true that he had worked hard for everything good that had happened to him.

But it was also true that he wasn't any more talented, hadn't worked any harder, hadn't done anything different than a lot of other men he played with.

God had blessed him.

The older he got, the more he saw it. The more he tried to appreciate it. The more he tried to talk to God about things instead of just doing everything his own way.

He supposed that's what he had done with Orchid. He chased after her without checking with God first.

But he felt at peace when he thought about her. He didn't think he was going in the wrong direction. Maybe he was just going about it the wrong way.

How can I know? What do I do?

He found a bench and sat. He didn't know for how long, his head down, his forearms resting on his knees. He wasn't afraid of hard work, he just needed to know what direction his hard work should take.

"I thought I saw someone out here," a voice said beside his ear.

He looked up to see a dark figure, not very tall, wrapped in what looked like a billowing cape.

"Miss Charlene?" he said, recognizing the voice but unable to make out her features or anything other than the dark material fluttering around her.

"That's right. My house is just down yonder. I happened to be up; I couldn't sleep. Something was nagging at me, but I couldn't figure out what it was. I looked out the window and saw a figure sitting here. Now, that I'm here and see it's you, I think I might know what had been bothering me." She adjusted her walker until she was standing beside him at the bench. "Is it okay if I sit down?"

"I hate to keep you out in the cold."

"We can walk to the church. It's not far, and it would give us a sanctuary from the wind."

"Can you make it that far?"

"I might be old, but I'm not entirely helpless." Charlene's words were a little brisk, but her tone held humor. He stood, and they walked slowly toward the church, silence slipping in like a comfortable old shoe between them. Easy and warm, it lay soft and he felt no great desire to break it.

"I think I'd rather sit in the sanctuary for this discussion, but you'll have to help me up the steps," Miss Charlene said.

He put an arm around her and held out his other hand for hers. "Let's get you up first, then I'll grab your walker."

She huffed, then took his hand, and they walked slowly up the stairs.

All the while, he was thinking he didn't really want to talk to her. She'd already basically told him he wasn't good enough for Orchid, and she'd pretty much refused to help him. He couldn't hold it against her. He'd tried on his own, and it had been an unmitigated disaster. It wouldn't have been any different if the Piece Makers had helped.

Maybe he should tell her she'd been right. He didn't have a problem admitting when he'd been wrong. Not usually. He just tried hard not to be wrong, because it was much nicer to be right.

Of course.

As he stepped into the sanctuary, he said, "If you tell me where the lights are, I'll turn them on."

"I think it will be easier if we sit here in the dark. Sometimes words come out in the dark that can't come out under the harshness of bright lights."

He couldn't argue with that, because he knew it to be true. So he helped her to the back pew and sat down after she settled herself.

It took her a bit to adjust herself, and he waited, not overly eager to hear what she had to say anyway.

Finally, Charlene spoke, her voice surprisingly soft and gentle. "I know I'm pushing in a bit, coming out here, asking you to talk to me. You don't have to tell me what the problem is." She hesitated. "I know you were sitting there for some reason. And I am curious as to what it was. But honestly, I asked you to talk to me because I have an apology to give you."

"An apology?"

He couldn't think of anything she would need to apologize for. Had he missed something?

"I don't feel like you owe me anything, just so you know," he added, a little hesitantly, because he couldn't believe she wanted to apologize. Maybe he should tell her that she had been right, but he was curious as to what she was going to say, and he kept his mouth shut.

"You came to me and my friends, and you asked us for a favor. Instead of doing everything I could to help you, I brushed you off. I treated you like an outsider. Like you weren't as good as someone who had grown up in Sweet Water." Her voice was low. It was obvious her apology was sincere. "I acted like Sweet Water was the only place that could possibly be right for Orchid. I insisted that you needed to do what I wanted you to do in order for you to get me to help you. How arrogant of me. Basically, I was playing God. And I'm sorry."

He'd been a little offended at the time. But he certainly hadn't been so upset that he felt she needed to apologize. Still, he could see what she was saying. Why she might have thought she needed to apologize.

"Just so you know, I wasn't going around holding any of that against you. In fact, as we were walking along the street, I decided that I needed to tell you that you were right."

"What?" Charlene said.

"You were right about Orchid and me. She, at least, doesn't think we belong together."

"Your date didn't go well tonight?" Charlene asked, equal parts surprise and tenderness in her voice.

He didn't even bother to ask her where she heard that he was going on a date with Orchid. It was a small town. Probably everyone knew it. By 6 o'clock tomorrow morning, all those people would also know that his date with Orchid had been a total bust.

"No. I had a good time, but...I guess she didn't. I wanted to go out again, ask for her number, and she said no."

This was where he was happy for the fact that there were no lights. If there had been, he might not have been able to say all of that. After all, it was humiliating. He'd been more focused on his disappointment, but when he thought about everyone knowing, it was embarrassing as well. And humbling, because he knew he wasn't good enough for Orchid.

"I see."

He could almost see Charlene nodding her head. The light was just bright enough that he could see the outline of her chin going up and down.

"The thing is she said she liked me. She wanted me to find someone who appreciated me. And I had thought the date went really well." He stopped, frustrated. He wanted to get up and pace, but he put a hand on the back of the pew in front of him and held it tight. "Obviously I was wrong. I don't even know where I went wrong, so I can't figure out anything to fix it. Which is frustrating. Especially since...I really like her. More than I've ever liked anyone before. She's...different. Different in a way that feels perfect to me."

"Do you want to tell me about your date?" She shifted just slightly. "I might be an old woman, but I was young once. I might be able to give you a few pointers."

"It's too late. She turned me down so many times and finally took a chance on me, and somehow I blew it. I don't even know how. I'm sure she's not going to give me another chance."

"But God might."

"I hardly think so. Feels like God's against me in this too."

"You mean Orchid isn't the right girl for you?"

"No. I actually do have a peace about Orchid. Like she is the one. That's not it at all. It just seems like God's put up roadblock after roadblock after roadblock. And when I try to push through them, nothing works."

"Maybe He put up roadblocks because He wants you to have Orchid, but not in the way you want to have her."

"Meaning?" He had no idea what she was talking about.

"You wanted to take her out on a date. Maybe that's not the way God wants you to get to know her."

"What other way is there?" That's what people did when they were interested in a member of the opposite sex. They went out on a date together. That's just the way it went.

"Sometimes the best way to find someone is to stop looking for them and put your eyes on Jesus. See the work he has for you to do and do it. Pretty soon, you look around, and there's someone working beside you, someone sweet and cute and perfect, and you start talking to her, because you're working together, pulling for the same goal, serving the same Lord, and then you gradually get to know each other and start liking each other more. You don't need to date. That's artificial anyway. Married couples work together, they spend idle time together, they cook in their house and eat together, not get dressed up and go to some fancy restaurant. You're not yourself there."

"I took her to a bar. We didn't really get dressed up."

"You took her to a bar?"

He didn't need the lights on to know that Miss Charlene's eyebrows had just bumped into her hairline.

"Yes?"

"Oh, son." Charlene's calloused hand came out and found his forearm, squeezing it, and somehow that touch made him feel a little better. Less alone, maybe. Or maybe it was the word "son."

His mom had been a single mom and raised him herself. When he'd been a teenager, she married again. His stepdad hadn't been super interested in another man's child. And soon they'd had a new baby and then another of their own.

He hadn't begrudged his mom her happiness, but he had definitely felt unwanted.

Maybe that was why he was always trying to push himself forward, show off, make sure everyone saw him. Because there were times he felt invisible at home, except when he screwed up.

"Maybe you better tell me about the rest of the date. I think, if you want to hear it, I might be able to give you some help."

"No. I think you're right. Orchid and I really aren't meant to be. It's just my feelings that make me think that the door would open if I went through it the right way. I have another year left on my contract anyway. I need to be in Houston next year."

"Unless you retire."

She'd remembered. He'd been thinking more and more of it, especially when he thought there was a chance with Orchid. But he might as well be playing baseball if there wasn't any reason to be in North Dakota.

"Yeah." He didn't bother to explain to her that he probably wasn't going to retire.

"Well, I can't help you if you won't tell me about it."

She squeezed his arm again. Maybe that was what opened his mouth, or maybe, it was because he knew he needed wisdom that he didn't have. He'd asked God for it, and maybe this was his answer—God sent him Charlene? He hadn't considered that, considered that God might send a person to help him become wiser rather than placing the wisdom in his head.

So he told her about the date as best he could, trying to be as objective as possible. Trying to make sure that he got the details right, that he didn't paint himself out to be better than what he was. Although he tried his hardest. And that was the honest truth.

After he finished, Charlene sat still for a bit. He didn't know what that meant, her silence. He found himself wishing she would say something, tell him that it hadn't been him. But if that were true, then there really was nothing he could do. So he quit wishing for that, and instead he prayed, *Lord, if there's something that I'm doing wrong, please show me.*

Then he braced himself, putting his hand over top of the old hand that gripped his forearm.

That seemed to be the signal Charlene had been waiting for, or maybe it just stirred her out of her contemplations.

"Can I be honest with you?" she asked.

Chapter 5

Patience and the ability to listen. Never give up. Pray a lot. - Cindy Mt Olive, MS

"I WOULDN'T WANT YOU to be anything else. And you don't have to worry about whether or not your words will hurt my feelings. I found in baseball that I can't improve unless I know what I'm doing wrong. I assume this—life—is the same way." Dwight was as honest as he could be.

"I missed that humble heart when we spoke earlier, because of my bias against you. You aren't from Sweet Water, would take one of the ladies I love here away. I didn't allow myself to look beyond the surface things I didn't want and look instead at your character and your heart and the things that matter. That's why I needed to apologize."

He grunted, because she'd already apologized, and he wanted to know not what was best with him but what he needed to improve. Whatever was good or okay didn't need to be fixed.

"I think you're trying too hard," Charlene said after a small pause.

What? He was trying too hard?

"What do you mean?" he finally sputtered out.

"I think your concern and your focus is *you*. How you come off, how she sees you, what she sees when she looks at you, and you're making sure that everything that you present to her is perfect. You want the attention, you want the accolades, you want her to see that."

"Yeah. I wanted her to see that she's getting something valuable when she gets me. That she's not getting some chump that's never done anything with his life."

He didn't necessarily mean that in a bad way. Like people who weren't All-Star baseball players were chumps, just that he'd worked hard and accomplished things, and he wanted his accomplishments to be front and center.

"I don't think you realize you're coming across as arrogant. Possibly a know-it-all. Definitely a show-off. And maybe a braggart. I'm not calling you those names, because I don't think that's who you are, but I do think that might be how you're coming across." Charlene's voice had risen in the middle of her little speech, but then it softened, and she said the last line gently, with care and concern in her tone.

Dwight sat there, stunned. Had he really been coming across that way?

He dug back through his mind, memories, things he said, the way he'd monopolize the conversation. He thought she was listening and enchanted. Had he been wrong?

"I'm not saying she's not interested in you," Charlene said as though she could read his mind. "And knowing Orchid as I do, she doesn't talk a whole lot. She does a lot of thinking. And that's fine. She probably appreciates you talking. But...there is a fine line."

"How could I find that line? What can I do to fix it? Fix myself?" There were probably books on the subject. But books could be so generic. He had a batting coach to help him with his specific problems. He could get the basics from a book, but once he got to a high level, he needed individual attention. Dating wasn't quite the same, but he wanted the same results. Perfection. As close to it as he could get.

"How many times did you ask her about herself?"

"A couple," he said automatically, and then he thought about it. Had he asked her how she was? If he had, he probably hadn't listened, truly listened, to her answer, his mind already whirling about what he was going to say about himself. What she was going to think about his answers, trying to be funny and cute and interesting and intelligent.

"I think a lot of times when we want to impress someone, we're always thinking about how we sound. Making ourselves sound smart. Intelligent and wise, so we can impress them. I think we spend a lot of time thinking about *me*. And there's nothing wrong with trying to improve yourself. I think that's part of the reason that you're going to be successful. Because you're interested in getting better. But when you're with someone else, your focus should be them. Especially, and in particular, a date. It shouldn't be about what did she think about you, it should be about making her feel valued and interesting and cherished."

"I opened the door for her. I could tell she liked that."

"Yes. And I'm guessing you didn't do it to show off or to score brownie points, but you did it to show honor and respect to her."

"I guess. I didn't really think about it. I just did it, and it made her smile, so I did it again."

"And that's exactly what you need to do. Notice her reactions. See what she likes. I don't think you should change yourself to be what she likes, but you can change what you do, as long as you're not changing the person you are. If that makes sense."

"Yeah. I think I see."

"Did you ask her where she wanted to go?" Charlene's voice was matter-of-fact, like she was a police officer getting info for an investigation.

Dwight hesitated. "No. Seems like when I ask that question, it's always answered with 'I don't care,' and whoever I'm with expects me to read their mind."

Charlene laughed, although he didn't find it particularly funny. "I suppose if you pay attention to her, eventually you'll know the places she likes to go, and it will probably make her feel valued and interesting if you can figure that out and say something like, 'Would you like to go here,' knowing that she enjoys the place."

That made sense. That he eventually would figure out where she enjoyed going. "I think I see. How could I tell that though? How do I figure that out?"

"You listen. You listen to her talk. When you see someone eating a hot dog, and she says, 'My mom made us eat hot dogs every night of my childhood, and I can't stand them.' Then you know she doesn't like hot dogs. But maybe in passing she'll compliment someone on a perfume that smells good to her, or she might say that she loves turtles, or you'll pass a deer in the field and she'll say that raccoons are her favorite animal. Just in casual conversation with her, you can find out so much about her. Then you remember those things, think about them, then use them to become more considerate."

"Because that's what this is, a lack of consideration?" He hated thinking he wasn't considerate, but he knew it to be true. Sometimes he just didn't think about how other people might feel or what they might want. It was especially hard when they were different from him.

"Maybe. Among other things. We all have multiple areas where we can improve. Don't get down on yourself."

He squeezed her hand. "I'm not getting down on myself. I'm used to hearing about my issues and trying to fix them. Just... The stakes feel higher here. Because I care. It's not just my job, it's...more."

"That's part of the reason I changed my mind, realized how wrong I was. When I thought about how many times you'd asked her out, gotten a 'no' for an answer, and yet, you didn't give up. You didn't nag her, or stalk her, but just let her know you were interested. That you liked what you saw. That rejection didn't change how you felt."

Maybe that was one of his strengths. It had to be. "I've found that persistence pays off. Sometimes persistence leads to a dead end too. And it's hard to figure out whether you're going toward that dead end until you hit it."

"I know. And some people will say she said no, so move on. There are times where you have to keep trying and times when it's time to quit. Regardless, sometimes you just have to wait and see what works."

"It's going to be hard to change my mindset. Because I guess I've been judged on my performance for so long, I feel like that's where my worth is."

"People look at you and admire you for what you can do. They like you for that. They're friends with you because of that."

"I know. And I resent it at times. But I can see subconsciously I had internalized that and that's what I was trying to use to impress her."

"Yeah. And Orchid is deeper than that. She goes beyond the surface. That's part of the reason I think that you'll be successful if you change your strategy. Orchid wouldn't have said yes to your date if she didn't see something there that she really likes."

"And then I went and completely messed it up by parading all the other things I thought would impress her."

"And you can fix that." Charlene's words were firm.

He took a breath and blew it out. He wasn't going to be able to ask her out on another date. Not only had Miss Charlene said that wasn't the best way to get to know someone, but Orchid would definitely never say yes again.

"I guess I'll be hanging out at the auction barn a lot, just trying to be around her."

"There's an Apple Festival at the church next Monday. Daphne is supposed to be making apple turnovers with Orchid. But Daphne called me earlier today and told me that she's struggling trying to keep up with taking care of her mom and the ranch and her daughter and everything that she needs to do. I told her not to worry about it, that I would find someone to take her place."

Dwight's heart leapt. He would have another chance.

"I actually called two other people, people I can usually depend on at the last minute to fill in, and no one could. It felt odd. It was actually what I was up praying about tonight when I saw you. The festival itself, and the fact that I might have to be on my feet making apple turnovers. Which I don't think I could do. But God was working on answering my prayer before I even started praying it. If you're interested in making apple turnovers next Monday with Orchid?"

"I sure am!" he said, and then he sobered immediately. "But that might not be enough time for me to figure out how I need to be different and to practice it. I don't want to screw up again. She might give me another chance, but she can't keep giving me chance after chance if I'm still the same self-centered person."

"You're ninety percent there. Most of it is admitting that there might be a problem, some people just can't do that. They look at themselves and see perfection."

"I don't have a problem with that. I guess I just have a bunch of others."

"We all have problems. Your entire life can be spent striving to be more like Jesus, and you're never going to attain perfection. However, the more you try, the better you get."

"Let her talk, listen to her, and don't brag." He let out a breath. "I think I can do that. Sounds easy, I just... I just want her to see me. And then my mouth starts going, and I forget that it's less about me and more about her."

"More about the way you make her feel." Charlene's words were soft. "I'm not saying people should live by their feelings. I actually don't think they should. But there are more than one or two men in the world who have character and integrity. If you find one who does, but they brag and show off, they're going to get passed over, because she's going to go with someone who makes her feel special and wanted. And I guarantee you, if you make her feel that way, she's going to go out of her way to make you feel the same. A good woman will. I suppose there are women who are self-centered and egotistical, just like there are men. Most of the time, if you start, she'll follow. And then, it becomes a competition, where you see who can do the most things to make the other person feel good. It's like a competition in the very best sense of the word. In a good marriage, it will always be like that. Where you never pass up an opportunity to make your significant other feel good or to do something kind for them and make them smile. And you see these opportunities, because you've taken the time to get to know your spouse, what they love, what makes them feel loved, and what they enjoy."

He sat thinking for a moment. "I need to know her, like I know baseball."

"Exactly. You didn't become good at baseball because one day you picked up a bat and hit a ball. You studied it, watched it, lived it, breathed it. You tore it apart and put it back together piece by piece, you read everything you could get your hands on, and you spent hours working on getting better at it. I don't understand why people think that marriage is any different. Maybe some people are naturally kind and naturally think of others. Or maybe they're just married to someone who is naturally easygoing. But for most of us sinful, self-centered human beings, every day it's a job to get up and not think about ourselves but think about somebody else."

"And every day we do that, we become more like Jesus." Funny how the teachings that he learned when he was little clicked into place with Miss Charlene's words.

"That's right. Not only will she feel loved and cherished, but you will challenge her to be a better person. That's the kind of person that you want to be with, someone who makes you better. But not someone who makes you better because you have to be."

He wasn't sure he understood that.

Miss Charlene sighed. "Because they're such a jerk that you have to become a better person in order to put up with them."

Chapter 6

Communication Skills and Listening to what your wife or husband is saying. - Barbara A. Kelley from San Antonio, Texas

DWIGHT UNDERSTOOD. Learning to live with and love difficult people made a person better, but that didn't make a beautiful marriage.

"If you're stuck in a relationship like that, you will become better. But your marriage will never be the beautiful picture of the relationship between Christ and the church that it was meant to be. Because it wasn't meant to be that one person has to suck it up and take everything. It was meant to be a beautiful relationship of selfless love and giving and serving."

"It's no wonder so many marriages end in divorce. We're certainly not taught that. Not in school, not in society. Not in movies, TV shows, anywhere."

"Right. Because who wants to do that? It goes against everything that you think you deserve as a human. In fact, we're told we deserve so much more. The thing is, God's way seems backwards, but when you try it, it works."

"Yeah. And it turns out that it's the world that's wrong, but the lies are so seductive. That you need to look out for yourself, that everyone else needs to make you happy, that you need to find someone who makes you happy, that if you're not getting what you deserve out of your relationship, you have every right to walk away."

"That's garbage. Pure garbage. For Christians anyway. Yet, it's what we hear every day, even in the church."

Dwight stared into the darkness. It was easy to see that most of his life had been about himself. That he'd never gone into a relationship thinking to be selfless and giving on purpose, thinking to love sacrificially, wholly, and completely. Would he be able to change it? He only had a couple of days.

"Maybe I shouldn't do the apple turnovers. I need to change a lifetime of bad habits. I can't do that in just a few days."

"But God can."

God could.

"And maybe, something we haven't mentioned is building a foundation. Just forget about dating and relationships, romantic ones anyway, and just focus on being her friend. Building a friendship. That's what the best relationships are built on. Knowing you can count on someone no matter what."

"That seems very basic, but I hadn't considered that. Dating doesn't really help develop a friendship."

"No. It doesn't. And don't be too hard on yourself. Some of us didn't have good examples growing up."

"I definitely didn't." He didn't want to go into his history. Lots of kids grew up with a single mom or a single parent. Lots of kids had stepparents who weren't real interested in kids who weren't their flesh and blood. Lots of kids had dealt with what he had dealt with. There were no excuses, just changes he could make to fix the problem. He didn't want to cast blame and stand around whining that his life wasn't as good as what it could be. He'd do what he did when his baseball swing wasn't as good as what it could be.

He'd fix it.

Chapter 7

If you truly love and respect the person you married. - Neleigh Allen Greeley, Colorado

"CAN I PET THE KITTIES?" Powell looked at Orchid, her big brown eyes pleading.

Orchid couldn't have told her no if she wanted to, which she didn't. "Please. They need people to pet them so when we want to give them away, they're tame and nice."

People were always dropping off their stray cats at the auction barn. Often they were pregnant when they arrived. As much as they could, if the cats were able to be caught, Orchid and Lavender used their own personal money to have them spayed and to find homes for them if they could.

The kittens were usually easy to place, but they had nine or ten spayed female cats running around the auction barn, just because people often didn't want an adult cat.

They both knelt down. Powell reached out gently with one finger, stroking down a white kitten's back.

Orchid was just about to ask her about school when a noise made her look up.

It wasn't unusual for people to be working at the auction barn anytime of the day; often Coleman was there from early in the morning until late at night. Whether he was moving animals, fixing gates and pens, cleaning and sanitizing, or even doing paperwork.

Typically, though, on Saturdays and Wednesdays when they had an auction, they didn't do too much extra work, just unloaded animals and sometimes even went and picked them up.

But the person coming toward her down the aisle wasn't Coleman.

She hated that her first instinct was to duck away when she recognized Dwight.

It wasn't that she didn't like him. She actually liked him more since they'd gone out, but there had been no doubt in her mind they weren't compatible. She did her best to try to have fun, even though hanging out at a bar wasn't her thing. She'd never danced in public before or sung karaoke, and everything felt odd and uncomfortable.

Still, she didn't see any point in sitting around upset that they weren't doing something she wanted to or complaining about the plans he'd made and the fun he was trying to have, so she'd thrown herself into whatever they were doing, trying as hard as she could to have a good time.

It hadn't been terrible, but it certainly wasn't anything she wanted to repeat. She supposed she could see how people enjoyed stuff like that, and it was fine. It just wasn't for her.

If those were the kinds of things Dwight enjoyed, they would have a hard time finding a middle ground, since it wasn't something she wanted to do on a weekly or even monthly basis. In fact, she didn't care if she ever repeated it.

Her unwillingness to go out again hadn't really been all that, though. It had been more the idea that he was very stuck on himself. And again, she couldn't quite figure out if it was just because he was trying so hard to impress her, or if he was really like that all the time. Just talking about himself and showing off. It was fun and funny in a way, but she knew if it was something he did on a regular basis, she would get tired of everything always being about him.

She didn't need to have everything be about her, and she didn't want it to be. She was definitely comfortable letting him do most of the talking, anyway, but she didn't particularly want to be married to someone where being with him every day was an exercise in becoming more like Jesus, because she constantly had to give up everything she wanted for him.

Still, she couldn't deny she liked him and felt drawn to him, and as she suspected, their date made that worse.

Hoping he would pass with her just nodding and giving him a small wave, she looked back down at the kitten that Powell was petting.

But Powell had heard the noise, and she looked up.

"What's that?" she asked, her eyes coming back to Orchid, obviously expecting Orchid to explain what was making the noise. Orchid had always made a point to take the time to explain in as much detail as Powell wanted everything that was going on.

Over the years, that had paid off, and Powell was a great help wherever they went together, whether it was the sale barn or baking cookies in the kitchen.

"That looks like Mr. Dwight, and he's pulling the pressure washer behind him. I'm guessing he's going to be pressure washing the loading docks, but I could be wrong."

By that time, he'd reached them, and seeing them both look at him, he'd stopped.

"That's exactly what I'm doing."

"Do you work here?" Powell asked, standing up, unafraid. She'd always been treated with loving care by all of the Baldwin family, and she felt just as much at home at the sale barn as she did in her own house.

"I do. Just started today."

Orchid knew her face showed her surprise. It was several seconds before she could control it.

"I work here sometimes too. Sometimes Mr. Coleman even pays me." Powell stated this like she was talking to a coworker. And technically, she was.

"That's great. Then you can show me the ropes tonight. Have you ever pressure washed anything? You could help me with that too if you want."

Powell shook her head, looking sad. "Maybe I can watch for a little bit?"

"You sure can. As far as I'm concerned, you can help, if it's okay with Miss Orchid."

"Sure," Orchid said, standing up and brushing off her pant legs.

"Mr. Coleman said I'm supposed to be spraying off the loading docks. And I have to admit I've never used a pressure washer before, so you'll have to bear with me."

Dwight looked at Powell when he spoke, which Orchid liked. He was giving her attention and treating her like an adult, which made Powell feel good and made Orchid feel like he was good with children.

He chatted with her as they walked to the loading docks, Powell walking beside him, peppering him with questions which he answered with a patience and thoroughness that impressed Orchid.

She trailed behind, watching them, loving the way Powell seemed completely at ease and how Dwight seemed to enjoy her company. They had guys who worked at the sale barn before who made Orchid uncomfortable when they were around children. They didn't seem to feel protective toward them and viewed them as more of a nuisance and bother.

Orchid totally understood that, because sometimes children did get in the way, and sometimes they were a bother. But they were little humans and they needed to be trained, nurtured and loved, taught and helped. Some people seemed to naturally understand that, and some people were far more interested in themselves and not being bothered than they were in reaching out and helping.

For as much as she felt like Dwight was a little stuck on himself, was a bit arrogant and maybe a show-off, he definitely had a good way with Powell.

They reached the loading docks, and Dwight stopped, looking around. "He said there would be a hose spigot around here somewhere."

"It's over here." Orchid started walking toward it, and Dwight followed.

"You need to take that hose," she pointed at the hose that was wound up on the hook on the pressure washer, "and screw it into the spigot."

She picked up the hose as she spoke, realizing too late he was bending over for it too.

Their heads knocked into each other.

Sharp pain rotated out on either side of her skull, and she let out a startled yelp.

"I'm sorry. I know I have a hard head. That had to have hurt."

"It must have hurt you too," she said, one hand gripping the hose, the other pushing on the spot where her head hurt.

"Are you okay, Miss Orchid?" Powell said, concerned.

Orchid tried not to be irritated with herself. Dwight was acting like he hadn't felt a thing, while her head felt like it was going to split wide open.

She could be tough like him.

She tried to be anyway. "I'm fine." She tried to mean it.

Taking a breath, she pulled her focus from the pain and onto what she'd been doing.

"So anyway, try not to headbutt anyone whenever you grab the hose, and you screw it into the spigot right here." She showed Dwight and then turned the water on. "You don't want to run it without water in it. I did that once, and it was an expensive mistake. You'll ruin it, and it will be unfixable."

"Got it. I do believe that Coleman might have mentioned something about that and used you as an example."

"That's lovely. I'll have to thank him later. I'm so glad I can provide an object lesson for him to use with the new hires."

He snorted.

"I... I didn't realize you were planning on getting a job here."

"I didn't realize I was either." He looked at the coupling between the spigot and the hose like there was something interesting going on between the two of them. Or, more likely, he didn't want to meet her eyes.

When he didn't say any more, she asked, "How long are you planning on staying?"

Now he did move his eyes to her, and if she wasn't mistaken, there was some hurt in his. She hadn't meant to insult him.

"Does it bother you that I'm here?"

Immediately she felt bad. Like he might have taken her statement like she was hoping he wouldn't be there long.

"No. I... I like you." That was the truth. The absolute truth.

"I guess I wasn't getting that impression. Not today. Not Thursday either."

"I'm sorry."

"No. That's my line. I talked to Miss Charlene. She pointed out a few things that I might have been doing wrong. I can't fix what's already done, but she made some good points, and I'm going to try to make some changes. Not that I'm trying to talk you into anything, I just thought maybe that would ease your mind about my presence here."

"Your presence is not a problem. I promise. It's just that...you're a professional baseball player. I don't know a whole lot about the sport, although you did teach me a good bit about it on Thursday."

"Sorry."

She waved that off. She hadn't meant that as a slam, but too late she realized it probably came out that way. "But I'm just assuming you're making a lot of money at your baseball job. You...aren't working here because you need money."

"No."

He didn't say anything more, and she wanted to press him. Make him tell her exactly what his angle was. What he was aiming for. Why he was here. But it seemed too self-serving. Like if she asked, he would think she was assuming he was there because of her. She couldn't think of a way to phrase it where it didn't sound like she was accusing him of being there just to be around her, and that seemed arrogant and conceited.

Finally, she simply said, "Why are you here?"

He was quiet for a minute, his one hand resting on the handle of the pressure washer, the other hooking around his neck.

Powell shifted, but she didn't say anything. Normally she was very good when adults were talking and didn't need to be the center of attention. In her mind, Orchid was begging her to continue to be quiet because she was so curious as to what Dwight was going to say.

Finally, his hand dropped from around his neck.

"I told you I talked to Miss Charlene. I told you she pointed out some things I needed to work on. She also recommended that instead of trying to impress you with any of my accomplishments, whatever they are, or anything else, maybe I should just do something where I would be spending time around you, not in a romantic sense but just...just so that we can be friends."

He hung his head and looked away, almost as though he felt like his words were lame, like she would laugh. And maybe to someone else, they might be funny. Might be desperate even. But she was charmed.

She hadn't looked him up online, but if the rumors around town were true, the man was a millionaire, and yet he'd taken a manual labor job and was even now getting ready to spray poop off the cement just so that he could have the opportunity to become friends with her. Not even with the promise of anything more.

That was a far cry from the impression she had gotten every time she'd been with him before. Where he was always trying to make himself look bigger and better, to push his accomplishments out there and show off what he could do.

When he said he was going to try to do something different, to make some changes, he hadn't been lying.

"Wow," she finally said. And maybe there was something in her tone, because his head jerked up.

"You don't think I'm the biggest dork you've ever met?"

"No. No, I don't."

There were a few beats of silence, and then Powell said, "Miss Orchid, aren't you going to show him how to run it?"

That broke whatever spell was holding their eyes together, and Orchid shook her head slightly, unable to believe that she'd actually been staring into his eyes like she was in high school, instead of almost thirty years old.

"Of course. He's never used one before, he probably wouldn't mind me giving him a little lesson."

"Not at all. I'd appreciate it. Coleman gave me the lowdown, but it's always easier when you see it done."

She flipped the choke lever, grabbed the pull handle, and gave it two good yanks before the motor caught.

She pushed the choke back down and grabbed the wand. "You squeeze this when you want a stream of water to come out, and you let go when you don't. And that's as simple as it gets."

"Got it."

"If you start in this corner, you'll want to try to squirt everything away from the wall, otherwise you'll end up in the other corner, squirting it all back at you."

She pointed on the cement where she meant, and he nodded his head, understanding exactly what she was saying.

"Thanks."

She smiled, handing the wand over to him.

He took it without touching her, and to her surprise, part of her was a little disappointed.

Chapter 8

Love and respect. - Anonymous, Thacker, Alabama

ORCHID'S PHONE RANG, and she met Dwight's eyes, then glanced at Powell. He nodded just a little, and she knew that nod meant he'd keep an eye on her. She would be fine—but when someone was working, they needed to be aware of where she was.

Pulling her phone from her pocket, she saw it was Daphne and took a few steps away.

Powell hadn't seemed overly concerned about her grandmother, but Orchid knew the infection in her knee replacement was serious.

Not only had it kept her off her feet for several months, but it had proved resistant to treatment, and Daphne's concern was that it would spread and become life-threatening.

Her mother, Renée, was more concerned about her inability to work and being forced to sit inside with her leg straight and propped up.

"Hello?" She glanced over her shoulder and saw Dwight and Powell deep in conversation.

She'd have to remember to thank him later for distracting Powell and allowing her to take this call.

Powell was definitely at the age where she was curious about what was going on, and Daphne was trying to keep her from worrying about her grandmother's health.

Orchid was all for that.

"Hey. Just calling to check on Powell. She okay?"

"She's good. We're at the auction house right now. We were petting the kittens, but now we're watching the new guy use the pressure washer. Actually, Powell is talking to him right now, and I'm watching them."

"The new guy?"

Yeah, she should have figured she couldn't get that one past her friend. "Somehow Dwight tricked my brother into hiring him."

There was a loud, telling silence on the other end of the phone. Although Daphne's reaction was probably much the same as hers. What in the world would Dwight need a job for? He was a baseball player, not a common laborer.

"He must be pretty desperate to be around you."

"I don't think so." She hadn't been sure what all to make of his declaration that he wanted to be friends. She was suspicious, for sure. But he hadn't pushed her. He'd never pushed her. She liked that he respected her while still letting her know that he wanted her. Chasing her, but giving her room to breathe.

It was appealing for sure.

"Come on. That has to do something for you. The man's a ballplayer, and I could be wrong about this, but I'm betting he doesn't have to work a day in his life if he doesn't want to at any job other than baseball. The fact that he'd hire on at your family's auction barn and...what did you say he was doing? Pressure washing stuff? Doing manual labor, just to be near you... Tell me that's not romantic."

She could admit she'd been flattered. Not even flattered, because that implied that what he was doing wasn't sincere. She had been charmed, well and truly.

"You're right. But I don't want to read too much into it."

"How can you read too much into that? I mean, the man could rob a train for you, I suppose, and it might mean more—"

"Or less. Since that's illegal. But I certainly wouldn't be flattered if he did something illegal for me."

"Right. I mean, could there be a bigger signal he could send?"

"So you think I should...what?"

"I don't know. Just appreciate the fact that this was pretty big. If you don't like him and aren't interested, that's fine, but you gotta give him credit."

"You're right. I just don't know what that means. I don't want to think about it." She tried not to smile as she looked over. "He's really great with Powell. She seems to like him too."

"Good. I hate that I'm not there. I hate that her life isn't stable right now."

"I'm trying to make it as fun as possible, and she hasn't seemed worried or upset."

"I knew I could count on you."

"Have you heard anything about your mom?" She hated asking the question. Because if it was bad news, she was just bringing the focus back on something that Daphne probably didn't want to focus on.

"They're giving her antibiotics through her IV. They're hoping that will knock the infection out, and then they're going to put a new replacement in. We're still looking at a long time."

"Well, don't worry about Powell. She'll be fine with me tonight at the auction. You know my sisters and Coleman, and Dwight now too, will all look after her. The whole town will make sure she's fine."

"I know."

Orchid could almost picture her friend with her eyes closed, relief easing the lines from her face. Her neighbors would pick up the slack for her daughter if they needed to. She could depend on them.

"Mom wants me to go home, but it's a long drive, and as much as I want to be home with Powell, I want to be here to hear what the doctors are saying, because she needs me. Plus, she has a tendency to downplay things."

"You stay. I know the drive is long. I'll keep Powell, we'll go to church together, and I'll make sure she gets on the bus Monday morning."

"You can hang out at the farm if you want to. You know you're always welcome. There are four-wheelers in the barn, and Powell loves to ride."

"It's supposed to be nice tomorrow too. Maybe after church, we'll take a picnic and a drive."

"She'd love that. Thanks for making this special for her instead of hard."

"My pleasure." Orchid meant that. She wanted children of her own, after she was married, of course. "This is practice for when I have children someday."

"I hope that's soon. Truly. You'll be the best mom."

"Because I have you as my example." Daphne had always made a point not to complain, and she did not make Powell the center of the universe, but she did make sure she knew she was loved, not just by her mother but by her Creator. That was probably the key to having a child who was well-adjusted and confident. Knowing that the Creator of the universe thought they were special and unique and had a powerful love just for them.

Orchid only hoped she could teach her children that as well as Daphne had taught Powell.

Probably Powell still wondered about her father, but Orchid had never heard her ask or lament that she didn't have one.

Still, in a small town like Sweet Water, where most of the other children came from two-parent families, there probably was some doubt.

"I'll call you with any news or updates, but the doctor said they wanted to keep her for at least three days, will that be too much?"

"Not at all. I can get her off the bus and put her on, make sure she gets her schoolwork done for as long as you need me to."

"Thank you so much. Oh, the doctor just walked in. I need to go."

"Take care. Let me know if you need anything else."

"I will."

Orchid swiped off on her phone, saying a little prayer for her friend and for Renée. Renée had been so patient and such a trooper. It had already been a long road with her knee, and it looked like it was going to continue to be a struggle.

God had a purpose for every trial, and of course Daphne, Renée, and Orchid all knew that. Sometimes it was just hard to see what the purpose was when a person was in the middle of their struggle. That's when faith came in. The belief that everything was going to work out for good. The confidence that God was ordering a person's life for their benefit and His glory.

If Orchid were in charge, Powell would have a father, Daphne would be home with her daughter, and Renée would not have been laid up for the last several months.

But then, she would have robbed them all of the opportunities to grow. To show God's peace and joy through trials. To have people look at them and see a little glimpse of Jesus. To encourage other Christians, and to allow those who might not be believers to see something amazing in their life and want what they had—Jesus.

Orchid shook her head at her thoughts. She didn't feel like she reflected Jesus at all most of the time. She forgot that was the purpose of her life. She lifted herself up, thought about herself, focused on what made her happy. She got so caught up in her wants and desires and the little dramas that went on in her life that she forgot it wasn't about her.

It was about Jesus. And about others.

"I don't think you were paying attention, but Coleman came and got Powell. He said they had someone who wanted to choose one of the kittens to take home, and he needed Powell to show him which one she wanted. That's where they are."

Orchid whirled around. She had been so lost in her own little world that she hadn't even noticed that Powell wasn't there anymore, and she hadn't realized she was staring off into space, gripping her phone tightly in her hand.

She took it and shoved it in her pocket, taking a breath. "Thanks. I'm sorry I kind of abandoned you with her."

"You didn't. I saw what was going on. I...also heard a little of your conversation." He paused for just a moment. "I didn't mean to, but I shut the pressure washer off when Coleman came, and I could hear you."

Orchid looked in the direction of the pressure washer. She hadn't even noticed he had shut it off.

"No. That's fine. I know you weren't eavesdropping." She wouldn't think that he would anyway. Why would he be interested in her phone conversation?

"It sounded like you were going to be watching Powell for a few days, and I just figured I would tell you that I'll give you a hand if you want me to."

"Oh. Thanks. I... I appreciate that. But I've had her a lot, not overnight necessarily, but I've pretty much been Daphne's main babysitter since Powell was born."

"She seems like a nice little girl."

"She's the best." She almost added that she wanted her children to be just like Powell. But she didn't. It seemed odd to talk about future children that she didn't have with Dwight, almost like it was a hint. She didn't want to be hinting anything.

"I... I was wondering if you had talked to the Piece Makers? Or to Charlene in particular?"

"No. Not lately. Why?" She tilted her head, feeling like the change of subject was rather odd.

"Charlene said that Daphne had told her that she wouldn't be able to help with the Apple Festival."

"Oh! I'd forgotten. She and I were supposed to do the apple turnovers together." She let her voice trail off as she thought about all the things she'd have to do by herself. Powell would be a help, but she would also be in school.

"When I talked to Charlene, I said I would help you."

It took about five seconds for his words to penetrate into the thoughts that were swirling in her brain. Then her head jerked to him, and her eyes opened wide. "Why were you talking to Charlene?"

He seemed to stumble a little bit, and his eyes dropped. Then, he lifted his head.

"I met Charlene on the street in Sweet Water. We walked to the church together and chatted on the way. I... I hope it's okay. I know she was going to tell you that Daphne had called her, but she probably just hasn't had time yet."

"No. She's busy organizing everything, I can understand that it might have slipped her mind, especially since she probably figured it was taken care of since she had you lined up to take her place."

Orchid could not be upset about that at all. She knew spearheading the festival was a lot of work, and the Piece Makers always made this one the very best it could be. Still, there were a lot of moving parts, and it was hard to keep track of everything.

Daphne hadn't mentioned it, and that was understandable as well. She had her mother she was concerned about, and then her daughter. Obviously, she had taken care of making sure someone would take her place, and she knew Orchid would roll with whatever needed to be done.

"Thanks. I was a little worried that it might be something you weren't overly excited about." This statement hung in the air while he seemed to gauge her response.

"I'm sorry." She tried to articulate what she was sorry for. She wasn't sorry for refusing a second date. She knew that was the best decision. "Sorry for making you feel like I didn't like you at all."

He hadn't seen Jesus in her. He hadn't seen anything in her but someone who hurt him. Who was just concerned about herself. Surely she could have been kinder. Friendlier. Less focused on herself, and more focused on the people around her.

Although she believed with every fiber of her being that she had the right to her own opinion and had the right to make decisions based on it, she also hated that decision had hurt him.

"You don't need to apologize. You didn't do anything wrong. But if you don't mind, I'm looking forward to working with you." He grinned a little. "Now, I better get back to my pressure washing, or your brother's going to feel like he's not getting his money's worth out of me."

The way he said that caused Orchid to narrow her eyes.

"Is he paying you?"

Dwight just grinned, then turned and walked back to the pressure washer.

That cracker head. She shook her head, turning and heading down the aisle toward where the kittens were.

He was working for no pay. She'd bet money on it. Still, when she got to Coleman, she was going to ask to be sure.

She couldn't believe it. Actually, yes, she could. But still, the idea that he was not just doing manual labor but doing it for no pay was crazy.

She smiled at that thought, as she heard the pressure washer start behind her, and knew that there was more to the man using it than what she had first thought.

Chapter 9

Love with commitment. - Colleen Hughes

DWIGHT GOT STEPPED on by a cow, squeezed against the fence by a different cow, kicked in the thigh by a steer, smashed his thumb to the point where he had to focus all of his energy to keep his eyes from leaking, but the crowning moment had been the hog that had bitten his leg.

He checked, there was just a small break in his skin just above his knee, his jeans had protected him, but his entire body was one throbbing, massive pain. And if his experience in sports was any indication, he was going to hurt a lot worse tomorrow.

Not to mention, the auction wasn't even over.

He'd figured out that he shouldn't follow an animal too closely, because they could throw a kick back. Thankfully, he hadn't been centered behind the animal, or the kick might have landed somewhere that would have hurt far worse than his thigh.

Still, he learned his lesson, and he made sure the big black cow he now followed stayed well ahead of him.

Honestly, the pain aside, he'd been having a good time.

He hadn't been quite accepted with open arms, exactly, but the fact that Orchid had so many sisters, and they seemed to be more accepting than the men, had worked in his favor.

Not that they were fawning over him like baseball fans might. Just that there wasn't a competitive need to prove himself before they accepted him kind of thing that there was sometimes with men.

He still felt like an outsider. Like he didn't really belong in Sweet Water. Or maybe he didn't really belong in the farming community.

That might be true, for now. But he could learn.

He actually found there was a certain amount of satisfaction and enjoyment from his work, even though he was dusty and hot and tired.

Hot despite the below freezing chill in the air outside.

He'd been based in Houston too long, and he was a little spoiled weatherwise. Below freezing was an almost unheard-of temperature for that part of the country.

Still, his work had kept him active and busy, and he wouldn't be cold until this evening when he quit.

"Is this the last cow?" Coleman asked, his words clipped and businesslike.

Dwight already figured out that it was Coleman's job to keep things moving. He didn't want people to get bored and leave, so the goal of running the auction was to keep something in the arena as much as they could and cut down on the amount of time that it was empty, ever.

But that did not mean that they wanted the animals to be rushed or scared. Coleman had explained to him before they started that moving animals too fast just led to someone getting hurt.

"She is. There are a couple of herds of goats and a man-eating pig."

Coleman had already turned away, but he paused, turning back with a small grin on his face. "You got bit."

"She took a small chunk." He returned Coleman's grin.

"A little initiation." Coleman's grin widened, then he grew serious. "You want to make sure you put some antibiotic ointment on that. I know, we don't like to do a whole lot of babying, but pigs' bites are notorious for getting infected. You don't want to lose your leg because of it."

"No. I'm partial to both of them."

"That's what I thought."

Coleman didn't say any more but turned around, following the cow off the scale and into the arena.

Dwight waited for Coleman to shut the scale door on the arena side before he opened it on the holding pen side. The next animal that they brought out would be able to get on the scale but not able to get off of it.

The whole setup was kind of cool, and when he wasn't moving animals, he had a good time watching to see how things worked.

He hadn't been watching things so closely that he'd missed Orchid, though.

She always had a smile on her face, and a lot of the time, she was walking beside Powell either talking or listening. They did a lot of laughing, and she seemed to really enjoy what she did.

He would have thought this was a man's world, but Orchid was grace and light and, kind of like her name, brought a bit of beauty into what was otherwise a dusty, dirty, and stinky job.

They went through the goats, taking several herds out, and when Dwight brought the pig out, he made sure he kept a wide berth from the teeth at the front.

Far be it for anyone to call him a slow learner.

Another hour had gone by, and there were just some old milk cows waiting to be moved down. The stands had cleared until there were only a dozen or so people left, and there was a crowd at the side of the building where the loading docks were.

Coleman had directed him over there, and he was waiting for a farmer to close up his trailer and pull away when Orchid's voice startled him.

"Coleman said you needed some ointment on a pig bite."

"Yeah." Coleman had said that. And while Dwight respected Coleman, he hadn't been in a big hurry to get it done. In fact, he'd kind of forgotten about it. He'd been busy.

"Had you done that yet?"

"No."

"You want to follow me?"

She waited, like he would actually say no or something. He jerked his head, laughing a little to himself.

Coleman must have asked her to give him a hand. He wasn't sure what that meant. Maybe that he had the brother's approval?

It wasn't like everyone in town didn't already know how many times he'd been rejected, and they probably knew about their disastrous date as well. Not because he had said anything, and he didn't really think Orchid was the kind who would either, but these things got out.

Maybe he shouldn't read too much into it. Maybe Coleman was just concerned about a worker's comp claim.

Still, he could have found someone else to give him a hand.

She led him to the back, where there was a bench against the wall. There weren't too many places for leisure in the auction barn, but this was one. Maybe for older farmers who still loved to go to the auction, loved to walk around the pens and see what was for sale, but needed to take a break and sit for a spell.

Seemed like a good place for a bench anyway, and when Orchid pointed to it, he sat without a word.

Despite the work of the evening, he could still smell her scent as he walked past her, fresh like flowers in spring. Honestly, he wasn't even sure what orchids smelled like, but he supposed since she had the name of the flower, she might find perfume that suited her.

He didn't know, it just reminded him of joy and faith, and he had to admit it was very alluring.

"I assume it's on your lower leg?" she asked as he sat down. He wondered why she'd been looking at him like that.

He allowed one side of his mouth to curve. Friends could flirt a little, couldn't they?

He set his hand on his upper thigh and slid it around to his jean's pocket. "Here."

He had to work hard not to outright laugh as her eyes got big. She swallowed hard.

She was cute, adorable really, but there was an attraction that stirred in his chest, and as she bit her lip, he had to work to keep his eyes lifted to meet hers and not settle on her mouth.

"I thought Coleman told me it was on your kneecap."

He wanted to laugh again at the concern that was in her voice. She obviously didn't want him dropping his pants in front of her. And it wasn't that he wanted to, it was just he was enjoying teasing her a little.

But he didn't want to go overboard.

"I'm just teasing you. It's right here." He touched his knee, then worked on pulling his pant leg up over his boot and knee.

She laughed, as he hoped she would, and didn't seem the slightest bit upset that he tricked her. "It's a good thing. I was just about ready to tell you that you could put this on yourself."

"You don't have to put it on. I can do it, although if you want to nurse me, I'll let you."

Her eyes, which had been watching as he pulled his pant leg up, waiting to see what she was dealing with, lifted to his. There was still humor there, but he saw something deeper, stronger, and he felt pulled toward that.

Maybe it was too much to hope for that she felt the same thread of attraction he did.

"Must have been one of the larger pigs. The boots would have protected the bottom part of your leg."

"Yeah. If she'd gone there first, I'd have been a little smarter when she tried to go higher."

"You'll be smarter for next time. You probably already were. Pain is a good teacher." She spoke while looking at his knee. She didn't touch it but fingered the ointment in her hand.

"Yeah. That's the truth."

Sometimes he had been slow to learn the lesson the pain taught, but not this time. He was getting old enough that he had a deep and abiding respect for anything that hurt. And things that might not have bothered him too much in his twenties had definitely started to make their presence felt as he topped thirty.

"Looks like you're going to have a nice bruise there. She pinched you pretty good, but there's just a small spot where she broke the skin. I'm betting it was more because of your jeans rubbing against it than her actual tooth, but you still want to be careful. Especially around here. Anything that breaks the skin has potential to be a bad infection, at least until you start to develop antibodies from working here."

"Really? You actually get immune to things?"

She shrugged. "I suppose. I've never had any trouble. I mean, we all get our vaccinations for things like tetanus, of course, but studies have shown the more you're exposed to dirt, the higher your resistance to it is. If that's true, we all should have resistance that's through the roof."

He thought of his mother's immaculate house growing up. There had been no dirt allowed inside, no pets either. He had allergies as a child, although he'd outgrown them. But it made him think.

Still, his entire career in baseball had been outside, so it wasn't like he hadn't been exposed to some dirt.

"I suppose I'm well on my way. I feel like I swallowed a gallon of dust today."

"Dust is better than manure," she said as she unscrewed the cap on the ointment.

"Where's Powell?"

"Lavender took her. We have another person who wanted a kitten, and while Powell hates to see them go, she also likes to be involved."

"I see." He remembered what Charlene had said about listening to her talk and not trying to push himself. He didn't want to ask anything too personal, but he wanted to know everything there was to know about her, and so he said, "Have you ever gotten infected from a pig bite? Coleman talked like he'd seen it before."

"No. Not that I know of. None of us have. But we've all heard stories."

She said it like it was the most natural thing in the world, so he had to say, "Maybe that's just because of what you do for a living, because that's not exactly common knowledge in the real world."

"Real world? Like I live in a story world, and baseball is the real world?"

"Sure. Everyone knows baseball is where it's at. That's where all the hunks are." He hoped there was enough humor in his voice for her to know that he was absolutely joking. And just to put an exclamation point on that, he said, "I actually like it here. I've had a good time tonight. Your family is pretty great."

She had some ointment on her finger and paused to look up at him as she leaned over. "Thanks. I definitely agree with you on that one. I have the best family. Even Coleman."

"Especially Coleman. He's a great guy."

"Yeah, I was teasing. He held the family together after Dad died."

He wanted to ask more about that, but she looked back down, and she dabbed at his knee.

He held his breath, not because it hurt, but because she was touching him.

"This kind of ointment shouldn't sting at all. It never does for me, anyway."

"It doesn't."

"Oh. I thought you tensed. I was afraid that I'd grabbed the wrong stuff, but I didn't want to panic and start reading the tube with you sitting there thinking that I thought I might have put some kind of skin-eating acid on you."

"The thought never crossed my mind. Plus, you have it on your finger."

"That's true, and I'd like to keep my fingers if I can."

He almost made a comment about how slim and graceful her fingers were, but not only did that seem like something a junior high boy would say, it also seemed too far out of the friend zone that they'd agreed to stay in.

For now.

He had no intention of staying in it forever. Or at least not attempting to break free.

"There. That should do it."

He reached to pull his pant leg down.

"Be careful. Don't wipe it off when you pull it down."

"Yes, ma'am."

She pursed her lips, hearing a touch of sarcasm in his voice.

She narrowed her eyes at him. "You need to take this seriously. I really think you're going to be fine, but I don't want to see it causing any problems for you."

That was a hint at his baseball career, one that was unmistakable.

"I'll take it seriously. I might be retiring anyway."

If there was a chance for him and Orchid to have something together, he most definitely would be retiring. Baseball didn't hold the appeal for him that it used to. He still loved the game, still loved to play, but there was more to life than the sport he loved.

She blinked when he said that, indicating her surprise, but she made no comment of her own.

He kind of wanted to talk to her about it, but again, that would be pushing. And currently, whatever there was between them, it really wasn't something they would naturally discuss.

"You have ointment like this at home?" She held up the tube she had in her hand.

"I'm staying with Bryce, and I'm sure he does."

"Take this. We have an unopened container in the office, I just checked when I grabbed this one. I'll feel better if you have it. As soon as that's healed up, you can give it back."

She held out the tube, and he stared at it.

Finally he reached his hand up and said, "Thanks." He took it from her, standing as she stood back and shoving it in his back pocket.

He took a breath, wanting to ask for something and yet unaccountably nervous. Or maybe it made sense that he was anxious. There had been plenty of times where he had asked and she had declined. He supposed at this point it made sense that he should probably expect her to say no.

But he wouldn't know unless he asked, and he hadn't gotten to where he was by not taking risks.

"I was wondering if you and Powell might want to do something with me tomorrow afternoon. I heard you telling Daphne that you would watch Powell, and you mentioned a picnic. I know a good spot on Bryce's farm."

She froze, her eyes on the ground, one hand in her pocket. He thought she was considering it, taking her time, and he couldn't blame her. Maybe she was wondering if he had an angle. He did, but he wanted to reassure her.

"I know you said we'd be friends. And that's my thinking. We just have a good time with Powell and keep her distracted from noticing that her mom and grandma aren't at home."

That's what he had heard her saying, and he understood.

"Okay. Although, Mrs. Brown's farm borders Daphne's mom's farm to the north. They have an old barn and a creek. We've gone there before, and Powell really loves it there. Daphne said we could take four-wheelers, and...have you ridden before?"

"Some." He and some buddies had gone four-wheeling a few times in West Virginia. He'd never owned a machine himself, but he felt pretty confident riding one. Especially since the rolling West Virginia mountains were far different than the flat North Dakota landscape.

"Would you be comfortable doing that?"

"I sure would." He'd take anything she gave him. Anything that helped him be closer to her. He hoped that wasn't being greedy and it wasn't making him too much of a beggar either.

He kinda thought she was thawing toward him, and he had to credit Miss Charlene for that. He'd been trying to put her ideas into practice. Shutting up about himself, not showing off, being willing to work at the bottom and put the focus on her.

"Then great." She didn't seem to know what to say, so he stepped in.

"I could pick you girls up and take you to church. Want to ride with me?" He tried to say it low and slow and the way a friend would. The way a friend who really wanted her to ride with him would.

Not like a man who was really attracted to her, who admired her character and calmness and compassion. Even though he was that man.

"Powell adores you. I know she'd love to."

He was happy Powell liked him, but that wasn't really what he wanted to hear. He tried to contain the disappointment that made his stomach feel like it was echoing with emptiness.

"And I want to."

She added that last bit quickly, then she turned around and walked away.

All the time they'd been standing there, animals had been still getting loaded on the trucks, and there was still a line of vehicles outside, if the headlights he could see through the small window beside him was any indication.

He needed to get back to work too, but he allowed himself the time to smile and feel a little thrill of victory. She said yes. Yes to spending the day with him, yes to riding with him, yes to church with him. Yes to a picnic.

Yes.

He loved that word.

Chapter 10

I think first and foremost you have to be friends first before you start dating because you will have hard times during your relationship where things will be tested and tested hard. If you have that foundation to hold you up, that best friend by your side you have a better chance of withstanding those hard times. - Cindi Knowles - Atlanta, GA

ORCHID'S EYES POPPED open, and she looked around the darkness in confusion. Where was she?

And then she remembered. In the spare bedroom at Daphne's house.

Even before she figured that out, her lips curved up into a grin, and it was hard for her to get them to do anything but keep turning up.

She stretched leisurely and quit trying to wipe the grin off her face.

She'd had a great time last night at the auction. Just working around Dwight, who hadn't talked much to her but who had worked hard and stolen glances her way as much as she had done toward him.

It had been nice to talk to him when she'd pulled him aside to put ointment on his bite.

She wasn't really worried about it. The odds of him getting infected were really low, but they were there, and it really could be extremely nasty, but it hadn't been necessary for her to supervise, and it definitely hadn't been necessary for her to do it.

She'd wanted to.

Just like she'd wanted to give him her phone number later, after the animals had been loaded and Coleman had told Dwight he could go home. She stopped him and asked for his number just in case something odd happened in the morning. She could save him a trip out by texting him.

When she'd done it, out of the corner of her eye, she could see Coleman grinning. She wanted to smack him, tell him to go mind his own business. She didn't stand over his shoulder smirking every time he talked to a woman. Of course, now that he was married to Sadie, it was a moot point, but still.

Dwight had taken her number and texted her right away, saying, **Just so you have mine too.**

She smiled into the darkness. Laughing a little at herself. She was definitely acting like a lovesick teenager. And she'd barely even talked to him.

Suddenly her heart was seized with a little bit of fear. Wasn't this what she was afraid would happen? If she spent too much time with him, her feelings would get involved, and then she wouldn't be able to make a good, rational decision.

No. He'd been different since he started working at the auction barn. The few days she'd seen him, he hadn't been the same person he'd been on their date. Or that he'd been before, when he visited the auction barn, trying to talk to her.

The fear that had pinched her heart eased, and she felt peace.

Before she could enjoy the feeling, her phone buzzed from where she had it plugged in on the nightstand.

Reaching over, she saw it wasn't quite as early as what she thought, 7:30. It must be cloudy out for it to be so dark yet.

Unplugging her phone and holding it up to her face so it unlocked, she smiled when she saw the text was from Dwight.

Maybe he woke up with a smile on his face as well. She hoped so. Mornings were her favorite time of day, other than maybe sunset, especially this time of year, when the sight of the sun was so welcomed.

How do you feel about sticky buns for breakfast?

Her smile never wavered as her fingers moved across the phone.

I feel good.

I'll bring some out.

I'll make bacon and eggs.

Be there in twenty.

Her eyes widened. If he was going to be there in twenty minutes, she had a lot of work to do if she wanted to be ready.

She texted back, **okay**, then threw the covers off and jumped out of bed, turning around immediately and making it. That was a habit that had been ingrained in her since she was a child. Making her bed the second she got up, that way the job was done first thing. It wasn't something that nagged at her throughout the day. It took five seconds, tops. And already she had something accomplished.

Tempted to put bacon on the stove before she got in the shower, she didn't want to burn the house down, and not just because it wasn't her house, so she took a quick shower, then went out and got bacon started on the stove.

She promised herself that she would think "just friends" all day, and then she would call Daphne in the evening and make sure everything she thought was right on. Daphne would tell her the truth, even if it wasn't what she wanted to hear. That was part of what made Daphne a great friend.

She had the bacon in the skillet, but it wasn't nearly done when she heard Dwight's pickup pull in.

She put her hand on her stomach, wondering why it tightened with nerves.

They were friends. Yeah, he made her smile, but they were still just friends.

Heading to the door, she opened it just as he had his hand raised to knock.

"Perfect timing," she said, grinning.

"Did I get you out of bed?" he asked as he opened the screen door and she stood back, allowing him to walk in.

"I was awake."

"I did get you out of bed."

"Maybe. But I like mornings. I'm happy to be up. So, you did me a favor."

He grinned. "I heard your sister Marigold talking to another sister, I wasn't sure of her name, but they said you were always up early. I took them at their word, but they were a little bit wrong, it appears."

"7:30 is early to most people. And considering that I didn't get to bed until after almost two o'clock this morning, I'm pretty proud that I was awake."

"Yeah. I actually thought it was quite an accomplishment for me to be up too."

"You're not a morning person?" She closed the door behind him, and he walked over to the table.

"I can be, when I walk into a kitchen that smells like this."

"I thought maybe you'd want to have a little revenge. This isn't the hog that bit you yesterday, but it might be a relative." She walked over to the stove, forking the bacon and flipping it over.

He was quiet for a moment, then he snorted a laugh. "I'm not used to people making jokes about my breakfast food and getting revenge."

She almost put a hand over her mouth. Maybe she'd shocked him. That wasn't exactly what she was going for. "I'm sorry. Are you still going to be able to eat?"

"Bacon?"

"Yeah."

"I'm not dead."

"That's a relief. I'm really not into zombies, although I do like graveyards."

"You do? That sounds a little strange."

"Not in any weird way, just because they're usually peaceful. And I make up stories about the people who are buried there. Or maybe not even stories, just think that they used to be where I was, and I'm going to be where they are someday, and what do I want the time between where I am and where I'm going to be to look like. You know?"

"Talk about big picture thinking."

"I know, right? Because then you set goals, and you need to come back down to earth to create the steps to make it to them."

"Or just bulldoze your way through. Sometimes I do that."

She didn't say anything, because she was thinking that maybe that's what he was doing whenever he was with her before. Just trying as hard as he could to get what he wanted.

She didn't have to wonder long, because he spoke again. "Maybe that's part of where I messed up with us before. I didn't have a very good plan."

She looked back at the bacon, using the fork to flip it over, careful not to splash the grease out. "If you want to get the full effect of your revenge, you might want to come over here and do this."

"Pretty sure that was a sneaky way of you trying to get me to cook my own breakfast," he said, even as he moved over and took the fork from her hand.

His fingers touched hers, and she almost forgot to let go of the fork. Forgot to laugh. And couldn't think of a single smart thing to say in reply.

Instead, she looked up at him, laughter on her face, and something else, something new and fresh and tender weaving around her heart, and she supposed she was looking just to see if she could tell whether he was feeling that too.

Maybe. His eyes crinkled, laughter obvious, and she liked that. She liked a man who was happy, even at some crazy early hour in the morning. Liked a man who could make her laugh. Wanted to.

Would that last? Sometimes people went out of their way to make a good impression first, and then they forgot to take care of the people around them and went off, trying to make good impressions on everyone else and neglecting the people closest to them.

She thought of Mrs. Brown and her husband, the people they would see later. They barely spoke to each other, and she felt like that had happened to them. That it had become less important to them to take care of each other and more important to impress other people.

She was pretty sure they didn't hate each other. They just acted like their spouse didn't matter.

"What?" Dwight said, his own look mirroring the look that must have been on her face.

She almost didn't tell him, and then she figured since he had asked, he must have been interested. "I was just thinking of the couple whose farm we're going to go to today. And how maybe they started out really liking each other, making each other laugh in the morning, but now... I don't want to gossip about them, but they just don't seem to care about each other anymore. And I was just wondering..."

"If I would be that kind of person?" he supplied for her, but he seemed to feel uncomfortable doing it, like he might have been being presumptuous.

"And me. Just wondering what it takes to continue to respect the person you're with. To put them first. To care how you treat them. How to know you're getting that kind of person."

"I guess you probably look at how a person treats their friends. Particularly their good friends or their best friends. If they take advantage of their friends and treat people they barely know better, they'll probably do that to their spouse too."

"That's a good point. I suppose it's similar to the idea where you're supposed to look at how someone treats their mom or dad or siblings, and that's how they'll treat their spouse."

She moved back so he could reach the skillet, checking to make sure it was turned down low.

She turned toward the refrigerator to grab some eggs.

"I think there's a lot of truth to that."

She had her hand on the refrigerator door when a thought struck her. Maybe she was challenging him, or maybe she was just curious. She didn't stop to think about it.

"And you have a good relationship with your dad?"

"I don't even know who my dad is."

She stopped, looking over at him, noting the studious lack of emotion in his voice and his focus on the skillet, like it took great concentration to flip bacon.

"That's sad. I'm sorry, but it is."

"There's nothing to be sorry about. And I really don't know anything different. I was a teenager when my mom married again. I had a stepdad who really wasn't interested in me. He had kids of his own, and he and Mom had two kids together. I was extraneous."

"I see." Her heart twisted. The idea that someone thought they were extraneous. A child. A teenager. Anyone. "And your mom never told you who your dad was?"

"We never really talked about it. I always got the feeling she hated him."

"No child support?"

"Not that I know of. No contact at all. I honestly don't know if he knows about me. I like to think he doesn't, since I've never had any contact with him at all. If he knows about me, he doesn't give a flip."

She gritted her jaw and swallowed through her tight throat. How hard. And sad. And no wonder he wanted attention. No wonder he felt like he needed to brag or show off.

She felt even worse for hurting him. She hadn't realized what his story was. Feeling like he wasn't wanted, feeling like no one loved him, feeling like no one cared would have made a huge impact on him.

It didn't excuse wrong behavior, but it certainly did explain it.

"Seems like around here, there's a lot of two-parent homes. You probably think I'm a weirdo now."

"No. I... I was just thinking that you probably had to excel in order to get attention. Maybe that's what drove you to be a great baseball player."

"I don't know if I'd say great. I'm okay."

"Really?"

Chapter 11

I'll have to paraphrase what my mom and aunties told me before my wedding... Even though a marriage is said to be 50/50, some days it may be 60/40 even 70/30, and marrying a military man it could be 90/10 quite often. Just remember at the end of the day, with the right person, it always evens out to 50/50. - Tonya Cutaran-Mathis Pensacola, Fl.

DWIGHT HAD GONE FROM pushing baseball on her, practically telling her he was the best baseball player who ever lived, to saying he was just okay.

"Miss Charlene told me I brag too much. I realized she was right."

"Maybe that was because of some of the hang-ups from your teenage years? Where you didn't feel like your stepfather really cared about you, and you had to do something to get attention?"

"I guess."

He probably didn't want to talk about it, and she couldn't blame him. He hadn't come here to have a psychological evaluation and be told the root of all his problems. And that wasn't really her job anyway.

Her job was...to see him as Jesus saw him. For one. And accept him as he was while still challenging him, somehow, to be better.

"I didn't mean to make things so serious. I was actually having a good time joking with you. I guess I like to think about things though. Figure them out. Figure people out."

"I'm pretty simple. I like baseball. I like bacon. And..." He looked up, still harboring a sadness in his eyes, but the corners were twinkling again. "I'd tell you someone else I like, but I can't talk like that today. I promised I was going to be just friends."

She grinned. "Maybe by the end of the day, you'll be sick of me, and you won't want to talk like that anyway."

"I'll take that as a challenge." His grin was easy, confident, and she liked that. There was a point where things became arrogant, but she could admire a man who was strong, who knew what he wanted, who would protect her, without expecting that there would never be some flaws in his personality.

The thing that impressed her the most was that he had said that he talked to Miss Charlene, she'd given him advice, and he was actually trying to implement it. A man who could be taught, who wanted to do better, was far better than a man who was convinced he was already perfect.

She supposed the same thing went for women. For anyone. A person had to be teachable in order to grow.

Once a person thought they knew everything, there was no hope for improvement.

She cracked an egg into a bowl. "How many eggs would you like?"

He told her and she said, "Once you're done with the bacon, I'll cook them in that skillet in the grease."

"That sounds good."

"If you don't mind, I'm going to run to Powell's room and get her up."

"I can hold things down here. It's been a while since I caught a kitchen on fire. I'll do my best."

"Nice. Because that would really ruin my day."

He laughed, and she left the room smiling, almost wanting to whistle. She had to tell Lavender she'd been right. He really was a nice guy.

Her opinion didn't change as Powell came to the table, and Orchid cooked the eggs, and they ate together.

They stuck the cinnamon rolls in the microwave, and the sweet cinnamon scent, along with the bacon, made the house smell amazing.

"I almost feel like I need a nap after that," Dwight said as he pushed back away from the table.

"Peyton really outdid herself with those."

"Owen said his mom was going to close the shop after she gets married." Powell spoke up from the other side of the table across from Orchid.

"Actually, I think they're planning on getting married today." Dwight acted like he'd just remembered he'd heard that. Orchid couldn't believe it wasn't the first thing he said when he walked in the kitchen. "That's what Peyton said this morning when I picked up the rolls."

"Really?" Orchid sputtered. Why hadn't he said? That was big news.

"I totally forgot about it, but I had planned on asking when I walked in if it would be okay if Owen came with us today. I think they're going to have just a short ceremony after church, and then they were going to leave on a honeymoon, just for a few days. Nothing big or pretentious."

"Wow." Orchid thought about some of the weddings she'd been to, where the bride had planned them for a year or even more in advance. Where they put everything together, spent a ton of money, and everyone dealt with months of stress and strain.

"Talk about low-key," she finally said.

"Yeah. They just didn't want a lot of fuss. Bryce isn't a big crowd kind of person, and even when he was a ballplayer, he didn't like a ton of attention. Peyton seems to be the same."

"Miss Orchid, please let Owen come. I like him, and I'll have someone to play with."

"Oh. And Kendrick. Both of them. I told her I thought it would be fine."

Orchid figured it was a compliment to her that he'd totally forgotten about the wedding and the kids he'd offered to watch when he walked in and started talking to her, but it amazed her that he had.

She nodded her head, trying not to look sad. It was hard, because her heart broke a little for Powell and her desire to have siblings. She and Powell had talked about it at times, but she never said anything to Daphne because she didn't want to make her feel bad. There were just some things a person couldn't change.

"Of course. I'd love it if Owen and Kendrick would spend the day with us. That'll definitely make it more fun."

They cleaned off the table, and Orchid sent Powell off to get ready for church.

"Thanks a lot for bringing the sweet rolls. I'd take something sweet over something savory for breakfast any day."

"I have to admit, I overheard that in a conversation between Peyton and Bryce. They talked about how you often stopped in at Peyton's shop, in particular when she had sweet breakfast items. She told me cinnamon rolls were your favorite."

She almost accused him of cheating, but that wasn't cheating. That was a sign that he cared about her.

Her mouth was open, and she stood with the plates in one hand and silverware in the other.

She didn't know what to say. Thank him? After all, he cared enough to find out and then to actually get her something she liked.

"Was that something Miss Charlene suggested?"

"Asking all my friends what you like?" He grinned, unrepentant. "Not word for word, but the basic idea was there. Taking care to find out what you wanted, and then to go out of my way to make sure it happened."

"I wonder if they want their kids to be at their wedding. Probably, right?" She hadn't even thought, but that would mean maybe Dwight and she would witness the ceremony, too.

"That was the next thing I wanted to ask. I told her what I was doing with you today, and that's when they said that they had been thinking about a small ceremony after church, if we'd keep Owen and Kendrick, and wanted to know if it was going to affect my plans. I didn't want them to postpone their wedding because of me. And they asked if you'd be there, too. They wanted you to feel welcome. I hope you don't mind?"

"I don't think women ever mind going to weddings. It's romantic and fun."

His look said he wasn't sure that she really meant that, but she did. She'd never been to a wedding that she didn't enjoy.

They finished clearing off the table, and then she went to get ready for church, dressing up slightly more than what she might have if she hadn't been attending a wedding afterward. Even if the wedding was casual, it was still a celebration, and she was excited for Peyton and Bryce. Both of them seemed like they deserved a happily ever after, and she hoped they got it.

Thinking back, she actually hoped she got her own happily ever after.

With Dwight?

She shook the thought out of her head. It was easy for someone to change for one day. Not as easy for the change to stick. Even though she understood why he was acting the way he had, and even though it made perfect sense to her, that didn't mean that she wanted to marry someone like that.

Although, if this new one was the real, permanent Dwight... She was definitely interested.

Chapter 12

I think the ability to forgive makes a marriage last. - Linda King from Australia

"I NOW PRONOUNCE YOU man and wife. You may kiss the bride." The preacher's voice held humor as his kindly eyes looked at the couple in front of him.

Beside Dwight, Orchid sniffed, and he turned his head to look at her more fully.

Yeah. She actually had tears in her eyes. He hadn't thought she was joking when she said women loved weddings.

"I thought you said you loved weddings," he said, just to tease her and to try to get her to smile. He was pretty sure the tears were happy tears, romantic tears, maybe, but he still didn't like them.

Felt like he wanted to do something to get rid of them.

"I do. Can't you tell?"

"No. Looks like you're crying."

She hadn't taken her eyes off the couple, and her smile widened. He looked up just in time to see the end of the kiss and Bryce raising his head. There was no doubt as his friend looked down at his new wife that he absolutely adored her. And the way Peyton looked said she felt the same way about him.

Had anyone ever looked at him like that?

Dwight was pretty sure he already looked at Orchid that way. Or at least, he caught himself wanting to.

Still, Miss Charlene's advice had at least gotten him to be able to spend the day with her, and it was easier than he thought to focus on her. To find out what she liked. He could flat-out ask. That had been a success. And he could listen to her sisters' casual conversations. That had been a success as well.

He supposed, through the years, he'd missed all kinds of things because of his preoccupation with himself.

He shook his friend's hand and congratulated him while Orchid hugged Peyton and told her how beautiful she looked.

Her eyes sparkled. Her smile was huge and genuine.

The thought went through his mind that she would be a beautiful bride, and he wanted to tell her that, and after their conversation at breakfast, he thought that maybe she might be open to the idea of extending their friendship into something more. But what Miss Charlene had told him about a solid friendship being the basis of a good marriage rang in his ears.

There was no need to rush things. As much as his feelings and emotions wanted him to, he wanted to make sure he built something that would last. He'd never built a relationship before. Not deliberately. It had always been something that happened naturally, and he supposed there wasn't anything wrong with that, exactly, but the idea that they would be friends, that they would set out to create a solid friendship, something that they could build more on, was one that resonated with him.

Mastering the fundamentals were essential to being a good ballplayer. It made sense that a relationship that was supposed to last a lifetime would need just as much care taken at the beginning, laying down and mastering the things that would enable them to build something strong and resilient.

Orchid's comments from the morning rang in his head. He'd seen plenty of people be like that. Friendly to people who could get them somewhere. Agents, in particular, who sidled up to athletes who might be worth a lot of money.

It was all part of the business, but it had rubbed him the wrong way then, and now he could see how that showed a total lack of loyalty and consideration to the people they already represented.

He supposed it took character to treat people the person was familiar with as well as or better than strangers. Everyone wanted to put their best foot forward.

It was easy to let down his guard and want to relax and be more like himself in private.

And probably there was nothing wrong with that, if the idea that being more like himself would mean he was more considerate and kind to others.

Not taking advantage of them, just because he knew he could get away with it, but rather thinking about them and doing more to bless and encourage them.

From somewhere in the back of his mind, the Bible verse about iron sharpening iron flitted across his mind. Even if nothing happened between Orchid and him, he wanted to be friends with someone who challenged him and made him think. Who made him be a better person.

And he wanted to be that for her as well.

"Are you sure you don't want Paisley to hang out with you guys today? I've already told her she could have the day off, but she said she'd be more than happy to take the kids off your hands if you guys were actually planning on a date or something." Peyton's words came to his ears as he finished shaking Bryce's hand.

She'd been talking to Orchid, but Orchid shook her head.

"I think Powell was really looking forward to getting to play with other kids. And Dwight's actually very good with her. He just has a knack with children. I think Owen and Kendrick will have a good time. And it will be nice for Paisley to have a break."

"I'm sorry. I'm a little nervous because I hardly ever leave Owen alone, and I love Kendrick. I'm just worried. Ignore me."

"Perfectly normal. You just took a big step, so you have that, along with the idea that things are changing a little bit, and you're doing something you don't normally do by leaving Owen. I promise we'll take great care of him."

"Thank you."

Bryce had moved a step closer and put his arm back around Peyton, drawing her to his side. She went willingly and stood as though she was made especially for him.

Dwight figured there were probably people who were meant for each other who didn't fit together beautifully, but Bryce and Peyton did.

His fingers tingled just a little, and he knew it was because he longed to hold Orchid. To see if she melted into his side the way his friend's wife fitted perfectly into his.

Or maybe he just longed to have someone who loved and respected him beside him.

Funny, when he thought like that, it gave him a great desire to be a man she deserved. To grow and become better.

Friends.

He wanted to be a good friend to her. That was where it started. Miss Charlene hadn't led him wrong yet, and he was going to assume that she wouldn't.

Chapter 13

Supporting your spouse in all things good. - Nola Asher

ORCHID ALWAYS ENJOYED church, and it was even more fun after spending the morning with Dwight and Powell. Even better when she was looking forward to a wedding afterward. A simple, beautiful wedding of two people who loved each other.

She had to admit she was really looking forward to their picnic that afternoon as they gathered up Kendrick and Owen after they hugged their parents.

Paisley, their nanny, had smiled, a little shy. Orchid figured she'd probably make a really good friend.

"If anything happens, I don't have any plans, so call me. If you need me." Paisley hugged both of the children.

"You're welcome to come if you'd like, but I understand it's nice to have a little time off."

"The kids have really been looking forward to it. It'll give them a break from me."

"Thanks. We'll call you if anything comes up."

She nodded, and Orchid took Kendrick's hand. The little girl seemed precocious and completely unconcerned about leaving her parents as she chattered about what they'd packed for their picnic.

Powell was practically prancing in place as Owen and Kendrick walked out the door with them.

Owen was a little quiet, he was a few years older than the girls, but Powell and Kendrick hit it off immediately, chattering like old friends by the time they pulled out of the church parking lot.

Dwight had been rather quiet, whether that was because he was listening to the children, or whether there was something else going on, Orchid wasn't sure.

She hadn't been talking much either.

Mostly because she was happy. She'd had a good time that morning, had enjoyed breakfast and driving to church. The message had been excellent, they'd been challenged to think about others rather than themselves. That a person's problems had a tendency to grow smaller as they stopped looking at themselves and started helping other people.

Orchid had tucked that in the back of her head to think about and wait for an opportunity to put it into practice.

Then, of course, the short but beautiful wedding. Someday, hopefully, it would be her.

In the meantime, she was looking forward to taking the kids and having a great day.

Actually, she was looking forward to spending the day with Dwight.

They went to Powell's house where they changed quickly and walked out to the barn.

"There are two four-wheelers, and they're exactly the same. The few times we've ridden before, they've worked really well." Orchid walked easily beside Dwight, the picnic basket in her hand, while he carried a blanket and a jug of water.

The kids ran ahead of them, Kendrick and Powell carrying kites, while Owen had a book in one hand and a fishing rod and tackle box in his other.

"Good to hear. I'm not exactly super mechanical, and if they break down, we'll have to call someone."

"Coleman can fix a few things, and if he can't take care of it, his best friend Nolt probably can." She smiled easily but noted Dwight seemed to tense beside her.

Maybe she shouldn't have mentioned her brother and his friend. Perhaps her comment might have made him feel like he wasn't taking care of her and she had to find friends of her own to help her?

She hadn't meant it that way, but sometimes men could be sensitive.

It wasn't that she had to walk around on eggshells in order to not offend him, but she wanted to be considerate.

"Or we could just sit there until you figure something out." She slanted her eyes over at him, joking a little and wondering if this was something he could laugh about, or if she was going to have to be seriously careful.

He gave a self-depreciating grin. "Was it that obvious?"

"No. I just suspected."

"Sorry. I guess I was a little bit annoyed, not with you, with myself. I'm taking a girl out, a *friend* out," he emphasized the word friend. "I want to be able to take care of her. Not have to have her call her brother."

"That's what I figured. I'm sorry. I wasn't being very considerate."

"You were being honest. I was being a dork. We will call your brother if the four-wheelers break down."

"Thanks. Let's hope they don't."

His smile was easy, and it made her feel good that he could laugh at himself. That he could recognize there was a problem and try to fix it.

"You know, you can call me out if I do something dumb," she said, hoping it sounded casual, like wanting him to understand that she knew she was just as likely to make a mistake or be inconsiderate as anyone else.

"I haven't had that experience yet." He shrugged his shoulders and gave her a glance. While his eyes were crinkled, there was humor on his face. "I can't imagine it happening."

"No. That's ridiculous. You're not allowed to put me on a pedestal. I make just as many mistakes as the next person."

"I guess I don't care."

His words made her heart beat harder. Could it be possible that she actually found someone who would love her despite her faults? Would he really look at her and see the very best, rather than the very worst?

Maybe it was just a new person kind of thing. Where once they got to know each other and his rose-colored glasses fell off, he'd realize that her faults really did bother him.

She tried not to allow the negative thinking to bring her down but instead went back to the mindset that she was going to enjoy her day.

They started the four-wheelers, with the two girls riding with Orchid, and Owen riding with Dwight.

"You better go first, since I'm not sure how to get to the Browns' from here."

"I can. It's not far. Five minutes or so."

She and Daphne had been there hundreds of times as they hung out together growing up. The Browns' two boys were a few years younger than they were. Old enough to be out of college and moved out of the house, although neither one of them were married.

They pulled into the Browns', waving to Mr. Brown who was walking into the barn as they passed. Orchid continued to the house. She was sure that was where Mrs. Brown would be. It had been a while since she visited with her.

They pulled up and parked beside the Browns' pickup, near the front walk.

"I'm gonna run in. Mrs. Brown's probably in the kitchen."

"If you don't mind, I'm going to walk out to the barn and introduce myself to Mr. Brown."

She didn't mind at all. Probably her smile gave her away, but she was thrilled that Dwight was going to get to know the neighbors.

She nodded, and their eyes met and held, just a fraction of a second longer than they needed to, before she turned away.

"Girls, you can let your kites sit on the four-wheeler while we go in and talk to Mrs. Brown." She had already strapped the picnic basket down on the front rack, and she gave it a glance before she turned and started up the walk, Kendrick on one side of her and Powell on the other. The girls chattered across in front of her, talking about the things they wanted to do, with Powell telling Kendrick all the times they'd been at Mrs. Brown's and how much fun they'd had here on the farm.

Orchid listened, smiling. The girls were so cute together. They were almost the same age, with Kendrick being a little younger than Powell, and they got along well and seemed to be able to find plenty of things to talk about. She wasn't sure they'd stopped chatting since they left the church.

Thinking how sweet it would be if the girls became best friends because of today, Orchid walked up the steps to the back porch and knocked on the door.

She'd been here enough to know that the Browns seldom used the front door. And definitely not for neighborly visits.

"Come on in. It's open."

Orchid opened the door and stepped inside the big country kitchen. Mrs. Brown sat at a large wooden table, a five-gallon bucket of beans in front of her and two more sitting beside her. A pan sat in her lap, and she held a knife in one hand and a long green bean in the other.

"Orchid! It's been ages since I've seen you."

"I know. It's been far too long." Orchid walked across the kitchen floor, glancing at the stove where large pots of water sat and at the counter which was filled with jars. When she reached Mrs. Brown, she leaned down and gave her a hug. Mrs. Brown raised the hand that had the bean in it, keeping the one with the knife lowered.

"It looks like you're busy today."

"I sure am. Mrs. Hanson gave me this huge crop of beans. She's getting too old to be able to put them all up, and I need to get them done before they go bad. I'd hate to lose them. With the price of groceries, we can use them."

"Wow. That's a lot of work." Orchid felt a bit guilty that she was going to go play and have a leisurely afternoon, knowing that her neighbor could use a helping hand.

"It sure is. I know I'm not going to be able to get it all done today, but I'm not getting anything done if I don't get started. So I sat down and got started."

Orchid nodded, looking around the kitchen again. "You don't have very many jars. Are you freezing some?"

"I might have to. My knee just isn't working well, and I was having trouble bringing the jars up from the cellar."

"I can go down and get them if you want me to. The girls can carry some too if that's okay."

"That'd be a wonderful help, but I'm sure that's not the reason you came."

"No. It's not. We were hoping that we could drive the four-wheelers back along your field and have a picnic by the pond."

"Of course. You don't have to ask."

"I hate to do it without at least letting you know."

"Well, you can rest assured you just let me know then. You don't have to get the jars. I'll figure something out."

"We'll do it." She looked back at the girls. "Won't we, girls?"

They nodded eagerly, like she figured they would. They were sweet girls, and most of the time, children had a heart to help, unless they'd been brought up to think that any kind of work was something to be complained about and put off. Neither one of these two had, which was as Orchid figured.

A lot of times, kids looked at work as just as much fun as anything else. Although, it was normally hard to try to put a good spin on doing beans, since most kids got bored sitting around, stuck in a chair, unable to get up and play.

Mrs. Brown told them where the jars were in the basement, and Orchid led the girls to the cellar door. She'd been down here a few times with Mrs. Brown, particularly in her high school years when she, Daphne, Lavender, and their other friend Katie had helped her some with cooking and canning and gardening.

It took six trips, but they brought all the jars up. Mrs. Brown was so appreciative, Orchid thought she might cry. She definitely had tears in her eyes, and she thanked them again and again.

They talked a little about how Orchid's mom was and Mrs. Brown's boys, and then Orchid thanked her and walked out of the kitchen with Kendrick and Powell.

Feeling guilty.

That was a lot of beans for one person to do alone.

She walked slowly to the four-wheelers, but Dwight was nowhere in sight. It surprised Orchid that he wasn't waiting since they'd spent so much time getting the jars. She thought for sure Dwight would be done talking and would be waiting on them.

"Let's walk over to the barn, okay, girls?"

"Yeah! I love playing in the barn." Powell grabbed a hold of Kendrick's arm and practically dragged her across the yard, chattering the whole time about how much fun it was to play in the barn, how there was still some grain in the granaries and how she loved wading through it, and how she played house in the hayloft.

Orchid smiled good-naturedly and followed more sedately, still wishing there was something she could do to help Mrs. Brown.

Maybe once they were done with their picnic, she could stop and help for a few hours this evening. Although she hated to do that to Dwight.

So, she did the next best thing and said a short prayer.
Lord, please send Mrs. Brown some help.

Chapter 14

Communication. - Twila Mason in Missouri

DWIGHT WALKED OVER to the barn, going to the side door where he'd seen Mr. Brown walking in as they pulled up to the house.

As they walked, Owen talked about the fish he'd caught down by the river, and then he said, "That's almost as good of a place to fish as the pond that we're going to go to."

"It's not very big, is it?" Dwight asked, thinking about the "river" they'd crossed on the little bridge as they came in. It didn't look much bigger than a creek to him, slow moving and not very deep. But it was flat North Dakota, so there wasn't much white water anywhere.

"It's not. But the fish bite, and that's all I care about."

Dwight grinned and gave Owen a look that said he understood. He enjoyed fishing when he was catching something. Although he got bored easily and usually only sat around for five or ten minutes before he ended up wading in the river himself and destroying any chance he had of catching any fish.

At least this river would be good wading. It didn't look like it was deep enough to be a swimming river.

He opened the door and held it while Owen walked in.

"Mr. Brown?" he called out to the deserted barn loft. There was a bunch of equipment scattered around and what looked like dressers and other furniture covered in drop cloths and sitting on the barn floor.

"Yeah? Someone call me?" a man called out before his head popped up from behind one of the dressers.

"Sorry. Didn't mean to startle you, but Orchid Baldwin and I were dropping in to see if it'd be okay if we take the four-wheelers down to the pond and have a picnic with the kids."

"Of course. She does that all the time, and it's always okay." Mr. Brown straightened up and came out from behind the furniture, walking toward Dwight with his hand out. "I know Orchid, but I don't believe I've met you before. I'm Stan."

Dwight took the proffered hand. "Dwight Eckenrode. Orchid is a friend of mine."

He silently added that he hoped she was soon more, but he didn't say that aloud. He didn't want to pressure Orchid, and he didn't want to get any rumors started flying around, any more than they already were, that he was pushing for more.

"Nice girl," Stan said.

"Yeah. She is." Dwight looked around the barn. "Looks like you're storing furniture."

"Yeah. I'm actually getting ready to load up my trailer. I've sold some of it, but I promised to deliver it myself."

"You have someone coming to help you?" Dwight asked, looking at the furniture, then back to Stan. It was a big job for just one person.

"My boys were supposed to show up, but the oldest one had some cows get out, and they're working on that. Can't hardly leave when your animals are out."

"No." Dwight hesitated. He wanted to stay and help. Hated to see the man trying to do this by himself, when he obviously needed someone, but the kids were expecting to go for a picnic, and Orchid was too.

He didn't want to cancel on them or even postpone it. Not unless they all agreed with him. And he wasn't sure he could ask them, since he wouldn't want them to feel like they had to say yes and then resent the fact that he didn't do what he said he was going to do and keep his word.

He looked around, realizing Owen was no longer beside him.

Glancing up, he saw that Owen was climbing the hayloft, trying to get to the girls who were sitting on a couple of hay bales in the middle of the loft. They must have come in a different door. He hadn't even heard them.

"That hay must be pretty old."

"It is. I haven't made any for ten years, but when I sold the animals, the fella didn't want the hay to go with them. They were just going to a feed lot and auction. I've never gotten around to doing anything with it." His voice held a smile as his eyes looked with indulgence at the kids playing. "Powell is here often, and she loves playing on it. I figure someday I might have grandkids, and they'd enjoy it too." He looked back to Dwight. "Guess I'll just leave it here."

Dwight nodded, loving that the man considered the hay in his barn to be basically a big toy for the kids to play in. He bet when Powell got older, she would understand how blessed she was to have a neighbor who enjoyed watching her enjoy herself.

"I better go see if Orchid's ready to go," Dwight said, although he wanted to offer to stay and help Mr. Brown. It looked like a big job.

Mr. Brown said goodbye and bent back down to do whatever he had been doing behind the furniture as Dwight turned away.

Orchid opened the barn door as he reached it, and he laughed. "I was just coming to look for you. The kids are all in here playing in the loft."

Her smile was small, and her brows furrowed like she was worried about something.

He reached out and touched her arm. "What is it?"

She bit her lip and looked up at him like she was worried about what he was going to say.

"Is Mrs. Brown okay?" he asked, pitching his voice low so he didn't alert Mr. Brown to any issues that there might be, at least until Orchid had told him what the issue was.

"She's fine. She's just swamped with work. She has three five-gallon buckets of green beans to do, and that would be enough work to keep five people busy all day. I feel guilty using their property to play on when she has so much work to do."

He let out a chuckle, which made her brows lift.

"I felt the same way. Mr. Brown is trying to get some furniture loaded, and he was hoping his boys would come help. But they have cows out, and they haven't shown up yet."

"Humph. Their cows are always out." Orchid shook her head. "Coleman actually said last Sunday at dinner he was planning on going over to their farm south of Sweet Water and helping them fix the fence. It's old. There are holes in so many places it's not even funny."

"So you're saying they might not make it today?"

"I don't know. I guess I wouldn't hold my breath about it." She hadn't stopped biting her lip, and now she wrung her fingers together as well. "I know we had plans—"

"I was thinking—"

They both stopped short, then laughed.

"I think we're thinking the same thing," Dwight said, and he couldn't keep the disappointment out of his voice. He had wanted to spend the day with Orchid. He enjoyed what they'd done together so far. And especially after the romance of the wedding, he wanted more.

But he loved that she had been just as convicted as he had. Maybe it had been the sermon, which had been about getting your eyes off yourself and looking around to help others. How that made a person's own problems smaller and the world bigger and better. Or maybe it was just her influence and how that was helping him to grow.

"I think we are too." She sighed. "The beans in the kitchen will take all day. Probably long into the night."

"I don't think the furniture will take that long. Maybe I can help when I'm done."

"What about the kids?"

He looked over his shoulder. The children hadn't even noticed that Orchid and he stood in the doorway or that he had been walking out. "I bet they'd be just as happy running around here all day, if the Browns are okay with that."

"I know they will be, although I'll say something. Especially if we are helping them."

"That's what I thought. Mr. Brown is letting that old hay sit in his hayloft, even though he could have sold it or gotten rid of it somehow, just because he loves to have it there for the kids to play on. He seems like such a nice guy."

"Mrs. Brown is the same. She's just a sweetheart." Orchid's eyes lowered. And her face took on a sad tone.

"But?" Dwight asked, wondering if she'd even tell him.

"They just don't seem to love each other anymore. It's weird. They're kind people, everyone loves them, but I can't remember the last time I saw them talking together. They're never with each other. Like today, Mrs. Brown has all those beans to do, Mr. Brown is out here with all his work to do, and neither one of them is helping the other."

"I see. I guess sometimes marriages just get stale."

"I guess they do. If you don't make the effort to keep them fresh."

Maybe that was a weird way to talk about it, like they were talking about a marriage like they were talking about bread. But he understood exactly what she was saying.

"I don't think it's either one of their faults. And I don't think there was any cheating or abuse or anything like that going on. They just...don't seem to love each other anymore."

"That's something you have to guard against in your marriage. Not that you have to keep staring into each other's eyes with stars in your own, just..."

"Exactly. You have to make a point to put your spouse first. To do little things to make them happy. To stop doing things that irritate them. You have to make a point to spend time together and enjoy each other."

"Yeah, I do know a few couples who have let themselves go, not in a physical sense, although that happens, but just they're miserable to be around, and they don't even realize how miserable they are. Sometimes I wonder how their spouse can stand to be in the same house with them."

"Maybe that's what's going on behind closed doors. I don't know. They've always been super sweet and kind to us whenever we visit."

Dwight nodded. He wasn't an expert on marriage or relationships or romance. Far from it. He'd obviously needed advice of his own to get to where he was, which was firmly in the friend zone. But sometimes it was easy to look at someone else's marriage and see little things they could do to fix potential problems.

Orchid didn't seem inclined to leave. Maybe she was as disappointed as he was that they weren't going to be together today.

After he'd been married twenty or thirty or fifty years, would he be that disappointed that he didn't get to spend the day with his wife?

"You know, people would say that communication is important in a marriage, but you know it takes two people to communicate. If one refuses, no amount of communication from the other can fix anything."

"Or when one spouse gets angry when their wife tries to talk to them. I played with a couple of fellas like that. Their wife could say something as simple as 'can you stop at the store and pick up milk,' and it would set them off, either on the phone with her or after they hung up. Like I don't know, maybe she did treat him like a slave, but it seems to me that if your wife can't ask for something as simple as a jug of milk without getting cut down, she's probably not going to talk to you about anything deeper."

He liked the way Orchid was looking at him, like he knew something important.

Not that he agreed with her necessarily, because obviously his track record in relationships wasn't that great, but he did know that if someone tried to talk, the other person had to listen and actually hear what they were saying. Not ignore them or get angry.

"There's no fixing things if you can't talk. And you're absolutely right. If one person isn't listening, all the talking in the world isn't going to make a difference."

She grunted and shrugged her shoulder apologetically. "I'm sorry. I'm putting this off. I... I was looking forward to spending the day with you."

"Maybe... Maybe we can do something later this week."

"I'd like that."

A thrill went through him at her words. He felt like it proved the things that Miss Charlene had said were completely right. He just needed to back off, stop thinking about himself, focus on her and just being a friend. Not about making himself look the very best he could.

It made sense, and he couldn't believe he hadn't seen it before. Sometimes he was dense.

Chapter 15

Love, Trust and Desire to "give in" to the wishes of the other person to help keep both of you on the road to Happiness! (It works because we have been happily married for 48 years!) - Jean Katchmar from Ellenton, FL

"IF IT'S OKAY WITH YOU, Dwight and I decided that we would stay here today, and I'll give you a hand with these beans."

Orchid stood in Mrs. Brown's kitchen, her hand on the counter, as she watched Mrs. Brown's eyes light up, then fill with tears.

"You don't have to do that!"

"We wanted to. Mr. Brown has some things to do out in the barn, and Dwight is going to help him with that. And the kids just love playing in the barn. They didn't even whimper when we said that we were going to stay here instead of continuing on like we'd originally planned."

"Well, bless your soul," Mrs. Brown said, smiling. "The boys were supposed to be helping Stan, but they had some farm work they had to do first."

"I heard about that. And that's too bad, but we can pitch in."

"That's so kind of you." Mrs. Brown nodded toward the cupboard. "There's a bowl in there you can use, grab a knife from the drawer and whatever else you think you might want. There's food in the fridge, but I was just going to have cold sandwiches and leftovers to eat for lunch."

"We packed a picnic lunch for the kids, and I'll just nibble when you do."

The last thing Orchid wanted to do was to cause more work for Mrs. Brown. The idea of her helping was to make things easier, not harder.

They had gotten through one of the five-gallon buckets of beans, and Mrs. Brown was knee-deep in a story from her childhood, talking about the house her mom had grown up in with her eleven siblings and no electricity until she was a teenager in high school, when Mr. Brown walked into the kitchen. He set the bucket he carried down next to the counter as Dwight walked in behind him.

"Don't set that there. It's muddy and will get the floor dirty. Set it on the rug." Mrs. Brown's voice took on a different tone, irritation and exasperation, and nothing like the tone she'd been using to tell her story.

Orchid bit her tongue. Mr. and Mrs. Brown never seemed to get along or spend any time together, and maybe that was part of the reason why. Orchid couldn't remember a time when Mrs. Brown had smiled at her husband and thanked him.

Maybe he deliberately tried to avoid her because he knew nothing he did would be right.

She threw the ends of the beans in the discard bucket and grabbed another whole bean from the pile, using her knife to snap the ends off and cut the bean into small pieces.

Without stopping her work, she said, "Did you guys get something to eat?"

She was mostly asking for Dwight, because she had been supposed to be spending the day with him and wanted to make sure he didn't end up starving when he thought she had been going to provide food for him.

"I thought about asking the kids to share their picnic food, but they seemed to be having a really good time up in the hayloft, and I haven't yet."

It was after one o'clock, and the man must be starving.

"Mr. Brown knows how to make his own food, and he can show Dwight, too. There are plenty of leftovers in the fridge." Mrs. Brown's tone wasn't quite as brisk as it had been, maybe because she was including Dwight in her invitation.

Orchid lifted her eyes, meeting Dwight's across the room. Questions in hers. She wanted to make sure he was okay with that and comfortable.

He grinned a little and nodded. She thought he understood what she had been asking, and she was pretty sure she was reading his answer right.

"We can grab something when we go to town. I don't want to take the time now. I want to get this stuff delivered before those clouds on the horizon whip themselves into something more than just a tease." Mr. Brown straightened and moved off the rug.

Orchid was happy that Dwight would at least get something to eat, although she was a little dismayed that they really weren't going to be spending any time together.

"If you don't mind, you said you got a text from your boys that said they'd be meeting you in town. So it sounds like you're going to have plenty of help to unload the furniture. I'll just stay here with your wife and Orchid and give them a hand with the beans."

Mr. Brown seemed very surprised at those words, but he jerked his head. "They said they'd be there, so I'm good. Thanks for your help. I couldn't have done without you."

He held out his hand, and Dwight took it.

"My pleasure. You can call me anytime you need something. If I'm around, I'll give you a hand."

"I hope you find what you're looking for," Mr. Brown said, prompting Orchid to wonder what in the world he was talking about. She made a mental note to ask Dwight later.

"Thanks. I found some of it." His eyes were on her as he spoke, and again, she wondered what he meant. Maybe she'd get a chance to talk to him alone, since he was staying.

That was kind of unbelievable. Normal people didn't choose to sit in a kitchen and snap beans on a beautiful day like today.

But he pulled up a chair, Mrs. Brown told him where the bowls were, and he watched what they were doing for a few minutes before he grabbed a knife and began.

"Cut the ends off first. Make sure they don't get in with the good beans, then cut the bean into pieces, drop it in the bowl, throw the ends away, and get another one. That's all there is to it."

"It's not hard, as long as you don't get the ends mixed up with the good beans. People get a little upset when they open up a jar and there's inedible stuff in it." She gave him a goofy look. "Ask me how I know."

Mrs. Brown laughed, and then she said, "Some people don't use knives. They just snap the ends off and then snap the beans into pieces. That makes my fingers sore, especially with this many beans."

"Same here. And I can do it faster with a knife. As long as the knife is sharp."

"The sharper the knife, the more likely it is I'm going to lose a fingertip." Dwight seemed to be only half joking about that, and while she laughed, more than once she'd cut herself and ended the day with several Band-Aids on each finger.

She held up the thumb of her left hand.

"I didn't quite lose a tip, but I lost some blood."

He grinned, although she thought maybe that serious undertone in his eyes was a little bit worried. "Looks like you took a chunk out of your bandage, too."

"Yeah. Normally it's the right thumb I have trouble with, since it's usually on the other side of the bean from the knife, but today this one's been getting in the way for some reason."

"Oh, is that what it's called, getting in the way?"

"The knife has the right of way, every time."

"And the sharper the knife, the more right of way it needs, yes."

"Something like that. You'd think my brain would get the memo, but as many years as I've been doing this, I always cut myself at least once."

"I, for one, appreciate your sacrifice," Mrs. Brown said with a small smile.

Orchid smiled, but in her head, she had to wonder why Mrs. Brown had changed so much when her husband came in the room. If she was as nice to him as she was to Orchid and Dwight, surely their relationship would be much warmer.

Things happened in relationships, hurts, slights, neglect. Maybe even betrayal. Things that were hard to forgive. She knew all that, but it just seemed hard to comprehend when both Mr. and Mrs. Brown seemed like such nice people. How could they not work it out and get along again?

The idea that they were too proud to apologize, both of them, made her sad.

But she shook it off.

It was shaping up to be a great day. Dwight was fun and funny, and she was enjoying his company. He made Mrs. Brown laugh, and her as well.

And by the end of the afternoon, they had all the beans snapped and ready for the canner. They had four batches finished and a fifth batch in the pressure cooker, with water heating on the stove so they could blanch and freeze some of them, since they were running out of jars.

Orchid stood, stretching her back and legs. It had been a long day. Her shoulders were aching and tired. Her hands were cramped from holding the knife, and she was ready to take a walk.

"I think everything's going to be good for a few minutes. If you don't mind, I think I'm going to get out and walk around outside for a bit. I need to move a little."

The kids had been in and out all day, but they had food and friends and a great place to play, so they hadn't seen them much.

Then, just an hour ago, Paisley had come to pick them up. When she'd seen what was going on, she'd offered to take Powell with her too, letting her stay overnight and sending her to school in the morning.

After a short text conversation with Daphne, Powell had been given permission and had eagerly gone off to stay overnight with her new friend.

"If you don't mind, I think I'll join you. I need to stretch my legs." Dwight stood from his chair, setting his bowl of snapped beans on the table.

"Of course, I don't mind."

If he'd been as funny on their date as he had been sitting at the table with Mrs. Brown, just chatting, cracking jokes, talking about anything and everything, she would have begged him for a second date.

As it was, she was wondering how she could ask him if he might still be interested. Maybe, after he'd gotten to know her, he'd decided that he didn't want to date after all. That would be the kind of irony that seemed to define her life.

After all, he seemed to be very happy with their agreement to just be friends.

"We won't be long, and you can text me if you need me," she said to Mrs. Brown as she walked to the kitchen door.

"Oh goodness, if you guys left right now, you'd still have helped me far more than I deserve. I appreciate it. I'd have been working on beans all week if it weren't for you."

"We won't leave until you're done. We'll be back."

Dwight had said something similar earlier in the afternoon, and Orchid had appreciated it. She didn't want to start a job and not finish it. Sometimes a person didn't have a choice, but when she committed to something, she liked to give everything she had and not back out. Not just because it was a part of her personality and a point of integrity, but because she had people who had done that to her before—bailed on her when she was depending on them.

She wanted to be the kind of person that people could depend on, not the kind of person other people were constantly wondering whether she was going to mean what she said or not.

They walked outside, onto the porch and down the steps. The sun was sinking low on the horizon, and it wouldn't be long until darkness settled down.

They walked toward the barn slowly, silently, just enjoying the glow settling on the horizon and the gentle breeze that drifted across the yard.

Reaching the fence that surrounded the empty corral beside the barn, they stopped, still without saying anything.

Orchid put her forearms on the top rail and rested her foot on the bottom.

Dwight turned toward her, leaning his hip against the post and shoving his hands in his pockets.

"Thanks a lot for staying. I know things didn't quite go the way we had planned, but..."

"It's like we took the sermon that was preached this morning and went out and put it directly to use." There was laughter in his tone, like he'd never done anything like that before.

"Funny how God worked that, wasn't it?" she said, never putting the two together until he just said something. "I had tucked it away in my mind, because I knew that was something I could use improvement on. I figured I'd think about it some this week and try to figure out what I could do."

"And you were doing it without even realizing it."

"Yeah. Not that I want any kind of pats on the back for it. I wasn't thinking about that. I just saw she needed help, knew we could do it, wanted to talk to you about it."

"Same with Mr. Brown. Maybe, sometimes doing right is less about deliberately making a plan and carrying out that plan, and more about gathering the knowledge in your head, until what you do naturally is what you should do, because you train your brain to think that way."

"Wow. That sounds a little bit like modern psychology. But it makes sense. You always hear that the Bible is powerful. When you read it, listen to it, hear it explained, it makes sense that it would change your brain. Change you."

"Exactly. Change you."

They were quiet for a bit, and while Orchid didn't know what Dwight was thinking, she knew she was considering how much she needed to change. How much she wanted to grow. How much she wanted to be better. And so often, she was trying to do as much as she could and was too busy to take time to do more than read a verse or two in her Bible, closing it and running away to do her good works.

"That kind of brings new meaning to the story of Mary and Martha and how Mary sat at Jesus's feet, and Martha was busy. Maybe Mary ended up accomplishing more because she had trained her brain first before she tried to do anything, while Martha was getting things done but maybe not the way God wanted or not the things God wanted."

"That's speculation, but I could agree with that. All throughout Scripture, God is clear that you accomplish more when you wait for Him, as much of a paradox as that is."

They stood in silence, thinking, but then he continued like he hadn't stopped. "I suppose it's a bit of a paradox, too, when you try to promote yourself and you end up doing the exact opposite. You have to wait and let God promote you. And then it means something. But a lot of times, the way He promotes isn't the way we think it should be done."

"It's like God lifting up the humble."

"That's right. There's power in humbleness, because it's God's power."

"God resists the proud but gives grace to the humble."

"And what can we not accomplish if we have God's grace and God's favor?"

She wanted him to keep talking. Loved listening to him, loved knowing that he believed what she did, that he brought out things she hadn't considered before, that he shone a light on them so that she saw them slightly different and had a deeper understanding.

But they lapsed into silence, and finally she asked the question nagging her since earlier in the afternoon.

"What did he mean when Mr. Brown said to you that he hoped you found what you were looking for, and you said you thought you found some of it?" She closed her mouth and then said quickly, "I hope I'm not prying."

Maybe it was presumptuous of her to assume that if he would tell Mr. Brown, he would tell her as well. Maybe they weren't as good of friends as what she wanted to think.

"I'm looking for a house. I found a couple, but they were sold before I made an offer on them. I was being too casual about my search, and the market's pretty tight right now."

"Oh. That's what you meant?"

"One of two things, I guess. I know where I want to live."

"Where?"

"Here. Sweet Water. It's the best place I've ever been."

"I haven't been very many places, but I have to agree with you. Sweet Water is awesome. I have no desire to leave." She gave a little embarrassed laugh. "I still live with my parents. Well, my mom. And I know that's kind of unusual, but our family seemed to bond after Dad died. Coleman was always a little different, maybe because he was a boy, and the oldest, or whatever. He was independent and didn't fit in as well, but for my sisters and I, we've all been very happy to stay home with Mom, working together."

"I admire that. Must be nice to have such a great family."

"Oh, it was. Not that we never fought or anything, I just know I never thought about moving out and getting my own place. It seems to be what everyone thinks you should do. But... Why not stay with your parents? Why not be with your family? Aren't you stronger as a unit?"

"You are. I wonder if that teaching is a little bit from the devil. Not that I think the devil goes around teaching things, but the Bible does say he goes to and fro over all the earth, seeking whom he may devour. Lions don't attack animals who are firmly in the middle of the group. They attack the ones who are alone. It makes sense that he can devour someone who's alone a lot more easily than he can get someone out of a group."

"Wow. I never thought of that. That... That is intriguing."

"Yeah. It wasn't something that was front and center in my mind either. After all, I've been alone for a long time."

"Since you moved out of your mom's house?"

Chapter 16

Trust, Honesty, and communication. - Caitlin Loggins, Hookdale, Illinois

"YEAH. THAT, AND MY mom was a single mom. I don't even know who my dad is. If she knows, she doesn't talk about it. But yeah, when she got remarried, I didn't really fit in with my stepdad. To be fair, I have to admit I didn't try. I got into a lot more trouble than I would have if I would have had a solid family behind me. Baseball kind of saved me. Maybe that's when I stopped being alone and started being with the group again."

Orchid hated that Dwight's childhood had been lonely and sad. That he'd longed for love. "Society is kind of breaking down all of those barriers where you have your family, your group that you're part of. Like that's a bad thing. It's really not. Not if the group you're involved in is a community of like-minded individuals."

"Like-minded is important for families. Businesses function well if there's a lot of diversity, although there still has to be something that strongly unifies it. But churches, families, communities function much better and are much stronger the more cohesive, the more similar they are."

"It makes you wonder how you fall for the lies."

"There are a lot of lies."

"You just have to hold things up to the light of the Bible. Scripture will guide you, but so often we want to throw it out, call it old-fashioned, and say it doesn't apply in our modern world. That God somehow didn't know."

"The Israelites would accept people into their community, but those people had to conform to what the Israelites believed and did. Look at how God commanded for them to handle people."

They were quiet for a bit, neither one of them seeming to want to continue that line of thought, because it was a hard teaching and not a fun one to think about. Which didn't make it any less important. Maybe more.

"In Genesis, God tells the man to leave his parents and cleave to his wife. If a man has already left his parents, he can't leave them. I suspect that that right there is a sign that children should be with their parents until they leave to get married. There is no command, but it does seem to make an assumption. And that goes back to what we were talking about before."

"About someone alone being more susceptible to attacks from the devil?"

"Exactly. If you have a young man or a young woman, say, in their late teens or early twenties, going off by themselves, with absolutely no adult supervision, they're much more likely to leave what they've been taught in their childhood and fall into sin. They are easy prey for the devil."

"It's scary, that is so true. But if they're still with their parents, they at least have that accountability. That knowledge that there is someone watching them."

"And then when they get married, they go from having the accountability to their parents to being accountable to their spouse. It completely leaves out that vulnerability of being alone. Where you don't have anyone you have to answer to, no one who sees the wickedness you're considering, and then trying, and then engaging in."

"'That digression,' Psalm one."

"Sure is."

"No wonder the devil pushes that age group so hard to want to be independent, get out from under their parents' care, and go off by themselves."

"The potential for falling into sin is huge, and the devil knows it."

She shifted against the fence, wishing she had an answer but knowing there was nothing she could do. "I hardly think we're going to change culture, although it makes me wish we could."

"God can."

She agreed with that, to a point. "He can, but it almost always takes something catastrophic. A flood."

Dwight snorted.

"Persecution of an entire people group," he said in much more serious tones.

She thought of the fact that Christianity had spread because Christians had been persecuted. And shuddered. "I started reading *Foxe's Book of Martyrs* once. I couldn't finish it."

"I know. It's hard reading. But that's how the early church spread."

"Yeah, that's a little scary. God has mercy, but a lot of times, there's a huge payment that's required."

Their conversation had turned extremely serious. The idea that persecution and hardship was the only way to bring Christians back to the Lord. When things were easy, people tended to have an easy, surface-only Christianity. It wasn't until things got difficult that they got serious about God. God had to manipulate situations, bring suffering and hardship into their lives, to drive them back to Him.

Orchid didn't want to be the kind of Christian who had to be driven to God. She wanted to be the kind who clung to Him voluntarily.

Unfortunately, far too often, she didn't think about the Lord until she needed Him.

"I think that's a pretty sober conversation. While I'm really enjoying it, I did kind of want to tell you that I really enjoyed my day with you today. I had fun."

She was relieved with his statement. She loved that she could talk about deep ideas with him, but she also loved that they could lighten the atmosphere. "You can be honest. Snapping beans is not fun for a lot of people."

"I can see how it would get boring. It's not hard work, just monotonous."

"Yeah. I've never had a problem doing monotonous work. My mind entertains me, but some of my sisters would rather pull their hair out in handfuls and clumps and roll over hot coals rather than be stuck in the kitchen snapping beans or shelling peas."

"Maybe it just depends on the company."

The sun had faded even more, but there was a three-quarter moon, and there was just light enough for her to see the flash of his teeth.

"I think Mrs. Brown's pretty awesome as well." She hesitated for a minute. Could she talk to him about their relationship? She didn't want to gossip, but she wanted to have the kind of relationship where both of them were aware of the pitfalls that could happen to couples who had been married for a long time. She wanted both of them to be interested in avoiding those.

One person could probably save a marriage by refusing to give up on it, no matter what the other person did, but that wasn't a picture of a beautiful marriage. It was a picture of someone who sacrificed in order to do right.

She didn't mind sacrifice, and she wanted to do right, but she didn't really want it to be what kept her marriage together.

"I wasn't talking about Mrs. Brown."

It took a minute for his words to penetrate her thoughts, and then she laughed. "I guess that's a compliment?"

"It sure is. I told you I had a good time with you today. *You*. Mrs. Brown... She's nice to know, but there's something...odd between her and her husband."

"I was wondering about that too. That's actually what I was just thinking. I didn't want to gossip or talk about them, but I wonder if there's something in the relationship that could be fixed. Neither one of them seems happy."

"Neither one of them seems to like the other one too much. After all, Mr. Brown could have been helping Mrs. Brown, and Mrs. Brown could have gone out and given Mr. Brown a hand. But it seemed like they couldn't get away from each other soon enough."

"That's sad. I don't think anyone stands at the altar on their wedding day thinking that's going to be them in twenty or twenty-five years."

"No. Absolutely not. And yet...there they are."

"It makes you want to help, but I have no idea what to do. And you really can't help someone who doesn't want it."

"No. But you can use them as an example."

They laughed softly and without much humor.

"An example of what not to do, you mean."

"Sure. There are good examples and bad examples. We can learn from both."

"They're both in the Bible."

She liked that he knew they could learn from examples as well. That he was interested in learning. So often people thought that love was easy. You fall in love, have the gushy feelings, and that was the end of it.

"As much as I love romance and the fun things to go with it, relationships are a lot of work."

"I agree. I've heard people say they're natural, but maybe that's when two people are completely living for the Lord and not being selfish."

"I think relationships would be perfect if we kept our eyes on Jesus and treated the other person the way we want to be treated. But yeah, that's pretty uncommon."

"So that's when they take work. When it's not natural to try to figure out what the other person wants or needs, and do your best to be that for them, while they are doing their best to be someone who's a blessing and help to you."

"That's the kind of relationship I want."

He pulled his hand out of his pocket and stepped closer, cupping her cheek.

She leaned into it.

"I know I promised we'd take it slow, and I want to honor that promise, but...that's the kind of relationship I want, too. One where we pay attention to it. Where it's the most important relationship we have in our life. We don't allow anything else to come before the other. Nothing other than God."

"And I think that's where God makes the relationship strong. You hear people saying you need to have three people in your relationship, each other and the Lord, and as you become a better Christian, more kind, more loving, more generous, less concerned about yourself, and more concerned about the people around you, you become a better spouse, a better mate, a better lover."

The last words were a little whispered, just because she wasn't trying to imply anything, just stating what she learned.

She appreciated that she could discuss things with him, and he could talk intelligently about them. He didn't just appease her, mindlessly listen to her, and then try to turn the conversation back to sports or walk away, uninterested and uninvested. That's what she'd been afraid of on their date. Part of it anyway.

"So much of life is all about that, isn't it? Getting the focus off yourself and onto others. And yet, from the time we're little all throughout our lives, pretty much the message we get every single day is that our focus should be on ourself."

She put her hand up to cover his, nodding and not wanting him to drop it.

"I don't see how a relationship could fail if both people are committed to putting their spouse first." She bit her lip. "But that's a scary thing. You can't control the other person. I have a friend, Katie, who married her high school sweetheart. Everyone said they were too young, but Katie is the nicest person I know, and I couldn't see how anyone could not love her completely. And yet, I'm not sure her husband's faithful."

"Ouch."

"I know. She's never caught him doing anything with anyone else, but she's kind and doesn't pry. And...he neglects her a lot."

He didn't say anything. What was there to say? She supposed she wasn't really asking for a discussion, as much as she was just telling him something she was afraid of.

"He promised to be faithful. She believed him. You can't make someone keep their word, and you really can't know if they're going to be the kind of man who does or who doesn't."

"Or woman."

"Yeah. Or woman. People grow, they change. How do you know that the man you married, or the woman you married," she added with a little smile, "is going to be someone who grows and changes in the right way? I mean, even preachers and pastors fall. There are no guarantees."

"No. There aren't. Maybe that's why love is so scary. Because you're taking such a big chance."

"Yeah. You're giving so much to somebody else, giving so much that's valuable and delicate and tender, and you can't be guaranteed they're going to cherish and honor it and keep it protected like God commands them to."

"You're opening yourself to the possibility of a lot of hurt."

"Yeah. Because the person that you're with is now involved intricately in your life. Your hopes and plans and dreams. They become a part of you."

"And when they play fast and loose with that, when they don't honor their word, don't put their spouse first, seek to serve themselves, and don't care about the disaster that their family will become because of their selfishness and neglect, it hurts. For a lifetime."

She wished she hadn't thought of Katie. Her heart hurt every time she considered her friend. She had beautiful children, a nice house, and was well-liked in the community, but it was also well known that her husband was not a man who could be trusted. He caused her a lot of heartache over the years, even if he had been faithful, which Orchid couldn't really say whether he had.

But looking at the man in front of her, there was a part of her that wanted to take a risk. That wanted to take his hand and walk further on. To trust him.

She closed the distance between them, lifting her hand and cupping his cheek as he did hers and lifting her face at the same time.

She hadn't really planned on doing that, but he leaned closer as well, and maybe she would have kissed him if her phone hadn't dinged with a text.

It startled them both, since the only sound had been the swish of the breeze through grass and the thumping of her own heart.

She jumped back, and his hand dropped, as did hers.

She fumbled for her phone, her breath uneven.

What was she doing? She was the one who had insisted that they had to stay just friends. And yet she was the one who had almost kissed him.

"Orchid, I—"

"It's Sadie. I'm picking up the apples early tomorrow morning at the auction barn, and she wanted to let me know that she would be there at six. She's getting one of their horses shod, and she was going to grab the apples on her way in."

Sadie and Coleman lived right by the orchard, and she would grab the apples in the morning.

She shoved her phone in her pocket, not wanting to talk about what she had almost done. "Mrs. Brown is probably waiting on us, wondering where we're off to."

"Mrs. Brown was young once."

His words brought her up short. Not necessarily what he said, but what it reminded her of. She had thought Mr. Brown and Mrs. Brown's relationship was in the state that it was in because they weren't talking to each other. And there she was, rushing off because she didn't want to talk.

Whether Dwight and she had a relationship, or whether it was just a friendship, she wasn't sure, but one thing she did know was that if it was going to be solid, she needed to resist the impulse to walk away without explaining.

"I'm sorry."

"About what?" His tone was truly baffled, although she suspected that even if he didn't have an inkling of what she was sorry about, there was probably at least a bit of irony floating around in his head that she was going to run off without talking, after they had just had a whole conversation about how important it was to talk.

"Because I was going to walk away without telling you why. Especially since you asked."

"Thank you. It does kind of make a fella think that maybe he shouldn't ask if he gets the silent treatment when he does."

"And it probably makes it harder to ask in the future. And then whoever you're with is going to accuse you of not caring because you didn't ask."

"I've been there."

"I have too. That's what I'm sorry about. And I... I was giving myself a hard time, because I told you I wanted to be just friends, and yet..." Could she admit what she had wanted to do? She didn't know how he felt, although he hadn't been backing away. He hadn't been putting up walls or trying to keep their conversation on non-intimate subjects.

She decided that part of their relationship depended on what they had just been discussing, taking a chance and trusting that God would order her life right, as long as she wasn't taking foolish chances or doing things just for herself, despite clear direction to the contrary.

"I was going to kiss you. I wanted to." She paused and hesitated for just a second, and then went all in. "I still do."

"I want you to."

Chapter 17

Communication. - Anonymous from California

"BUT I GOT SCARED. I questioned myself. After all, we were going to go slow. That's not slow. That's not friends. That's not anything that we decided. That's emotions." Orchid hoped Dwight understood and didn't think she was being silly or, worse, playing games.

"Emotions aren't all bad."

"But they often lead you to places where you shouldn't go."

"They do. But I don't think we should shut them down completely. Emotions are what makes us human. Emotions are part of what makes it so fun and exciting to be human."

"But emotion should come after rational thought. You shouldn't lead with them."

"Are we?"

It was a simple question, but she stopped, looking at him, her eyes fastened on his chin as she pondered that.

She didn't think they were, actually.

"I have a confession."

"Well?"

"I went to the Piece Makers. I asked them to help me find a match."

"You did?" She couldn't keep the shock out of her voice.

"A specific match."

She waited. Her breath frozen. Her hands clenching at her side.

"I wanted you. I wanted them to help me get you to be interested in me."

She had known he was interested. The whole town had known he was interested.

"It wasn't necessarily an emotional decision, although I can't deny I've had feelings for you for a long time. But those feelings are based on what I see in you. You consistently help your family. You're at the sale barn every time I am. You never shirk your duty. You're always doing more. You're always smiling, with a good attitude, making other people smile and laugh as well. You're a joy for people to be around, and everyone loves you. Now, the love of everyone isn't necessarily something that shows the mark of a good person. Lots of people are loved not because of their character but because of something fleeting and transient and shallow. But your joy is deep. And so is your integrity. That's not my emotions talking. That's my rational brain."

He pushed off from the fence but stepped aside, not closing the distance between them but bringing them so they faced each other.

"Maybe it's an emotional thing for you, and I don't mind that. But I hope you can find some kind of character, some kind of steadfast loyalty, some kind of something good, maybe a glimpse of Jesus, in me."

She realized he was right. There were emotions involved. She did feel pulled, but she had found plenty to admire about him too. And she knew from experience there were no guarantees. God wouldn't give her a guarantee. There just weren't any.

He gave guidelines. And examples. And that was the thing, she would be linking her life with someone else who was a sinner, saved only by grace, and also given free will.

She stepped closer to him, reaching up again, only this time with both hands. "You're right."

"I don't think I've ever heard those words before. Go ahead and say them again."

"You should listen closer the first time," she whispered, her eyes only partially open, her mouth smiling as the words left her lips.

He grinned a little too, and he seemed to have the same problem with his own eyes not wanting to stay open as his head lowered.

"Should I wait for a minute in case you're going to change your mind?" he asked softly.

"You can if you want to. But I'm not going to. And maybe I'll beat you to it anyway."

She lifted up on her tiptoes and pressed her lips against his. His arms came around her, pulling her closer, and she pressed into him.

The night sounds faded, the breeze a distant touch, the night black and far off.

He felt solid and strong, and she wanted to be closer, but he pulled back before she was nearly done.

"You are perfect," he said low with a note that almost sounded like longing in his voice. His forehead leaned against hers, and he took a couple of breaths. "But even though I feel like it's okay to give your feelings room, to let your emotions breathe, I also promised you we'd go slow. It won't make any difference if we do, other than I'm going to spend a lot of time dreaming about you."

Maybe she would have laughed if she hadn't wanted so badly for him to kiss her again.

But she knew he was right. They wouldn't regret waiting. Not if things worked the way they wanted them to.

She would, however, regret rushing ahead, going too fast, making their foundation sloppy and slipshod.

"I don't like what you just said, about waiting. But my affection and desire and admiration for you just grew immeasurably because of it. If that makes sense."

"And that's not your emotions. That's a rational reaction to my rationality."

They chuckled a little, and then his hands slipped down her back and lingered for just a moment at her waist before they fell completely away, although his left hand caught her right hand, and their fingers twined together.

"Let's go back to the house and finish these beans. Tomorrow is a big day."

"It is. But I'm looking forward to it."

Chapter 18

Constant communication, talk to each other all the time. Can't go wrong.
- Lyn Morris, St Helens, UK

IT WAS STILL DARK WHEN Dwight pulled into the auction barn the next morning. He hadn't gotten home the night before until after midnight, but the beans were all done, Mrs. Brown was happy, and most importantly, Orchid had been smiling when he left her.

She'd beamed as she pulled the last jar out of the canner and set it down on the counter. He felt a sense of accomplishment too, unexpected. Snapping beans without Orchid would have been a terrible job. As it was, he would have to say it had been one of the best days of his life.

Orchid was sweet and funny, as he'd always known she would be, but it was the first time he'd gotten to experience it firsthand and in such close quarters. He wanted more.

The day hadn't gone the way he had planned, not even a little, but God's intervention had made it so much better.

If he would have been able to choose, he would never have chosen to can beans, but that work had provided the perfect backdrop for Orchid and him to build a little on the foundation of their relationship.

He might slowly be coming to agree that dating was not the best way to get to know someone. But working with them, seeing how they reacted to the little bumps, a broken jar in the canner, one of the kids coming in with a bloodied finger, cutting herself with a knife, and dropping an entire bowl of cut beans on the floor, all those things showed them what kind of people they were, what kind of character they had, what kind of grace they were willing to offer.

He wouldn't have found any of that out on a date. A date was a manufactured time, a bunch of fakeness and superficiality that did nothing to show anyone what someone did in the real world, other than possibly how generous they were in their tip. And how they treated their waiter.

As he closed the door to his truck, he walked toward the bright lights which were on in the auction barn, with the big doors open. There was a horse cross tied in the walk.

Although he'd heard about him, he hadn't met the farrier, who, from what he understood, was an Irishman who had been hired by Ford Hansen when Ford had rescued a retired racehorse.

Looking around, Dwight did not see Orchid, so he stepped into the far entrance and stopped.

"Good morning," he said to the farrier who was bent over the hoof of a sparkling bay horse.

The man looked up, his emerald green eyes glinting in the light. "Top o' the morning to ye," he said with a grin that showed straight, white teeth. "Folks call me Tadhg."

There was a bit of stubble on the man's face, but he was the kind of fellow that girls might find handsome, Dwight supposed. He definitely had an easy grin and a cheerful way about him that put a person at ease immediately.

"I'm Dwight."

"You must be the bloke the lass was telling me would be coming." The man gave him another glance, then looked back down at the horse's hoof and ran a tool along the bottom of it. A thin piece of hoof shaved easily off. "She said to send ye in the direction of the office."

"Thanks."

The sale barn was sprawling, with lots of pens and aisles, but Dwight had been there enough by now that he knew the general direction he needed to go, found a set of stairs, and made his way to the office.

There were a few lights on, although it wasn't lit as brightly as it was on an auction evening.

The door to the office was open, and Sadie stood with Orchid beside the desk.

"I saw him with my own eyes, and that kiss was not the kind of kiss that a man gives a friend or coworker."

Orchid looked up, her eyes probably drawn by his movement in the doorway. "I don't know what to do. Let's think about it. I mean, someone's going to have to tell her. But I don't want it to be me. I'm sure you don't want to, either."

"No. I don't. You know her better than I do. You're probably the closest friend she has in the world, but I'm the one who saw him." Sadie looked at Dwight, then she jerked her head. "If you need me to go with you, text me."

"I will. Thanks for the apples."

Sadie waved at Dwight, and he waved back before he put his arm around Orchid, who had walked over to him and had seemed to have wilted since last night.

He waited until they were down the stairs and walking down the aisle before he said, "Some kind of bad news."

"The very worst."

They greeted Tadhg but didn't stop until they'd walked out to the parking lot. He had parked beside her car, and they stood in front of both vehicles.

Orchid turned toward him, and to his surprise, she stepped forward, wrapping both arms around him and laying her head on his chest.

He wasn't sure what the problem was, but he was happy with the direction things were taking. He held her tight, stroking down her hair, wishing that it hadn't been bad news that caused her to turn to him.

"Oh, Dwight. I don't want to do it."

"Can you tell me?"

"I told you about Katie last night. I mentioned her husband. I... I didn't know. It was coincidence, honest."

"What was?" he asked after she didn't say anything more.

"Sadie just told me she saw Katie's husband, Russel, meeting a woman at a gas station where she and Coleman had stopped for fuel when they were bringing their horses home from the show. She said she saw them get out of their cars, and the woman, whom Sadie didn't know, ran to him, they kissed, not a friendly kiss, and then she got into his car. They drove away."

Her body shook, like she was sobbing or holding back sobs. He held her tighter, put his hand under her hair, and stroked her neck.

"Wow." He didn't know what else to say. "And now you need to tell her."

"Someone has to. I would be so angry at my friends if they saw my husband do that, if they knew he was not being faithful to me, and they didn't say anything to me. But I suppose like everyone else in the world, I don't want to be the one who bears the bad tidings. She's not going to like this information. It's going to destroy her, going to blow up her family, even if she and Russel are able to work this out, she'll never be the same. I don't want to do that."

"You aren't. He's the one who did it."

"You know what they say about shooting the messenger. He is the one who did it, but I'm the one who's going to cause her pain. As long as she doesn't know, it doesn't hurt."

"And you said yourself, you'd want to know. As your friend I'd want you to know. I'm not just saying that. It's wrong for a married couple to keep secrets and sneak around behind each other's backs. If you can't be a man of character, you don't deserve to have a woman who is. That's just the way it should be."

He tried to tamp the anger in his chest down. It was true. How many times had he been with men on the team who were away from their wives and got away with things that their wives would have divorced them over?

But no one told. Everyone kept secrets, and marriages stayed intact. Not because the men had character and integrity, but because there was a brotherhood where they didn't tell on each other. It was a bunch of bunk, and he hated it. So unfair to their wives.

He'd always tried to focus on the game, but there was always a certain amount of comradery among his teammates. It helped build the trust and brotherhood necessary in order to win games.

Still, he hated seeing the cheating and the silence, because it was disgusting to see marriages built on such rottenness. He had vowed not to do it himself.

Maybe that was part of what attracted him so much to Orchid. Because she didn't seem to know or care that he was a popular sports figure and certainly wasn't interested in him for that. Although, baseball would always be a part of him. He was pretty sure she knew it and would support that, like she would support anything he did. And him her.

That was part of being in a relationship.

"I'd offer to go with you, but I assume my presence would be worse than not having anyone."

"It would be better for me, but it would probably be harder for Katie. This is going to be the worst thing she's ever been through."

"And there's nothing you can do to make it easier."

"No. But her parents have been married for fifty years, she's the youngest of seven children, and all six of her siblings have had lifelong marriages." Orchid grunted. "As far as I know, she'd be the first divorce in her family. I know this is going to devastate her."

He didn't say anything, just held her tight. Anger bubbled in his chest, and he tried again to push it down. It just made him so mad. People were so inconsiderate. They didn't think about how their actions were going to devastate others. Break up families, rip an innocent, faithful woman's heart out. She would never be the same. He just wanted to grab her husband and smack him against the wall.

"I guess it's a good thing I'm not God. Because men who did that kind of thing to their wives wouldn't survive."

God forgave. He forgave anything. Right now, in this moment, it was almost inconceivable. Dwight certainly didn't feel the slightest bit forgiving toward Katie's husband and didn't want to give him mercy or grace. Both of which had been extended to him.

That kind of thinking probably wouldn't help the situation for Katie. Not right now. Katie didn't even know and was certainly not ready to think about mercy and grace and forgiveness.

"How about I take the apples to the church, and I'll get started paring them and chopping them, and you can show me what to do. And then... Do you want to tell her now?"

Orchid let out a sigh and held tighter to his chest. "I think if she gets her kids on the bus... I'll try to time my arrival at her house right after that. That will give her the longest amount of time without them to process and recover."

"I thought the kids got out at noon today for the festival?"

"Yeah. I guess I was thinking that I would volunteer to take them and watch them at the festival. Maybe my sisters will help me."

"I can help too. Either with the turnovers or with the kids." He wanted to be someone she could count on. Even though he'd never made an apple turnover in his life before. While Orchid had shared the recipe, he was still a little fuzzy about the whole process.

Starting with how to turn the stove on.

But if it would help Orchid out, he would figure out what needed to be done and do it to the best of his ability.

"I appreciate it so much," she said against his chest.

They stood like that for a few more minutes before Orchid seemed to reluctantly pull away. "The apples are in the back of my car. Tadhg helped us carry them out and put them in."

"I'll follow you to the church and carry them in from your car, then you can go whenever you need to."

"Thanks."

Her hands seemed to cling to his waist for just a moment more before they dropped and she walked away.

A thread of anxiety slithered around his ribs. After their conversation yesterday, he knew this was one of her fears. That her marriage wouldn't last. That something like this would happen. He hoped that seeing what Katie was going to be going through, experiencing it with her, wouldn't keep her from taking this step with him. He could see how that could hurt. Having your best friend go through something like this would have to give a person second thoughts, especially if they weren't entirely sure to begin with.

Lord? Timing?

He knew God's timing was perfect, but sometimes, he wondered. Certainly this wasn't happening when he would have it happen. Actually, he wouldn't have something like this happen at all. Not to a woman who had been faithful and true.

They got to the church. He carried the apples in like he promised while Orchid was stopped by one of the Piece Makers, who wanted to talk about the number of turnovers she was planning on making.

Dwight opened the door with one finger, carrying in all three bushels of apples together.

He grabbed it with his foot and shoved it open, looking up in time to see one of the Powers brothers.

"Excuse me. Almost ran you over."

"You have your hands full. Here, let me hold the door," the man said. "I don't think I've ever introduced myself, and I'd offer to shake now, but it might be funny to watch you trying to juggle those bags of apples."

"Yeah. I'm sure you'd get a kick out of that. I'm Dwight."

The man had slipped through and held the door. "Good to meet you. I'm Brawley, one of the Powers brothers."

"I figured. Recognized you as a Powers, anyway." He stopped, looking into Brawley's eyes, and got struck by something...familiar.

He didn't mean to, but his eyes narrowed.

"What? I have something on my face? Guess I left without doing my regular beauty routine. It is kind of early."

"No," Dwight said absentmindedly. "There's nothing on your face, you just look...familiar."

"I look like my brothers. Although, the rest of them have brown eyes, and God gave me green for some reason."

They weren't an emerald green, but more of a sea green, like the Atlantic Ocean on a February day. Interesting. Because he'd just seen eyes that color not that long ago. Exactly that color. Eyes that had a slight tilt to them, the same tilt he saw in both sets of eyes.

He shook his head. What he was suspecting could not possibly be true. The whole town would know it. It wouldn't be just him.

Although, sometimes a person didn't see things that were right under their nose. Sometimes the best place to hide something was in the most obvious place, where no one would think to look for it, because it was too obvious.

Dwight shook his head, mumbled his thanks, and strode into the church.

"Good morning, Miss Charlene," he said, setting the apples down carefully on the table. He didn't know a whole lot about cooking much of anything, but he knew that apples bruised easily, and so he was careful as he handled them.

"Good morning. I see you arrived right as Orchid did," Miss Charlene said with a knowing look.

"I sure did. Thanks for setting this up so we could be together today."

"I've been hearing that you were together yesterday, so maybe you didn't need our services after all."

"I needed your advice. It's been working for me, and it made sense. I...don't want to lead her on with some kind of false pretenses. I don't want her to fall for me because she thinks I'm someone I'm not. And your advice helped me see that I was actually going about everything the wrong way."

"Sometimes we just need a little guidance. I got to thinking about what you were saying, and I also felt a little bad for the things I made you promise."

"What's that?" he asked, straightening up, glancing around the kitchen, and then looking at Miss Charlene more fully.

"I made you promise that you wouldn't take her away. Dwight, that's really not my place. If you're meant to be together. If God wants you to be together. You need to go where God wants you to go. Whether it's Sweet Water, whether it's somewhere else. That's the important thing, not doing what I want you to do."

"Thanks for the apology. Thanks for letting me off the hook for that, but I have no intention of taking her away. I just haven't found the perfect place to buy yet. I'm working on it." He grinned.

"You have a baseball career in Houston, and if you need to go, you have my blessing."

"Thanks. I'm pretty sure I'm gonna retire. I need to make a decision, but not today. Today, I'm gonna learn to make apple turnovers."

"You've never made them before?" Charlene asked, although why that information would surprise her, he had no idea.

"Surely you know men do crazy things for women they're interested in."

"I do know that. I guess occasionally I get forgetful in my old age."

"Well, yeah. I know how to eat apple turnovers, but that's pretty much all I know how to do with them."

"It's a good thing you have Orchid here to show you."

"Actually, Orchid has a visit to make before she can help me."

"She does?" Charlene said, her voice sounding thoughtful and curious. But to her credit, Charlene did not ask him what Orchid was doing. "That's good. Because I actually was looking for a job. I can give you a hand."

"I'll take it," he said. He'd rather have Orchid, but Charlene wouldn't mind teaching him how to make apple turnovers.

Chapter 19

I'm still trying to figure out what makes a marriage work, but I've only been married for 56 1/2 years, so time will tell. - Carol Collett from Iowa

AS SOON AS DWIGHT TOOK the apples out of her car and walked away, Orchid called her sister Lavender.

Back in the day, Orchid, Lavender, Katie, and Daphne had been inseparable. They remained friends as they become adults, even if they had gone in separate directions. With Katie getting married, Daphne having a child, and Orchid and Lavender working at the sale barn.

Lavender agreed to meet her, and she'd barely gotten off the phone with her when it rang with Daphne's number coming up.

"Hello?" she said, wishing Daphne could go with them. There was strength in numbers, and this was one of those times where Orchid was pretty sure Katie would appreciate having her very best friends in the world around her.

"Orchid, I just talked to Paisley, and she said Powell was up with Kendrick and Owen, and they were eating breakfast. She said they had a great time yesterday, and I just wanted to thank you."

"My pleasure. We had a good time, and although the plans we had didn't quite pan out, I thought everyone had a good time anyway."

"I can say for a fact that Kendrick and Owen had fun with Powell."

"That's great."

She wasn't sure whether to tell Daphne what was going on or not.

"Also, I'm on the way home. I'll actually hit Sweet Water in another fifteen minutes or so. The doctors were in doing rounds early this morning and decided that Mom could be moved to the smaller hospital in Rochester. They think she should only have to stay there a night or two before she's discharged. She'll still not be allowed to be on her leg at all, not even a little, but beyond that, they think she should be fine at home."

"That's great news!"

"Yeah. So, when Mom heard that, she insisted I go ahead of her, spend some time at the festival, and she said maybe I could bring Powell in later to see her or just come in tomorrow. She insisted she'll be fine."

"Doesn't she have a sister in Rochester or something?"

"Two, and yeah, they'll be there to visit her and take care of her. I have to say, I'm so glad to be going home. I miss Powell. I've never been away from her for that long, and I hate the big city."

"We all do. And sounds like the festival is just what you need."

"I was supposed to be helping someone make apple turnovers today."

"Well..."

"What?" Daphne asked, hearing that tone in her voice as good friends always did.

"Maybe you could help me. With something else. First."

"I don't think I'm going to like this."

"You're not. You're not at all."

Instead of telling her over the phone, she did the same thing she had done with Lavender, which was tell her that she would explain everything to them when they met at the C-Store in Sweet Water.

They spent a good thirty minutes in the parking lot at the C-Store crying and hugging each other after Orchid told Lavender and Daphne what was going on.

At last, they reluctantly got in Orchid's car and drove to Katie's house. Their timing was almost perfect. Five minutes after they pulled in, the bus came, swallowing up Katie's children and leaving them alone with their good friend.

Katie, bright and chipper as she always was, smiled with pure joy as she looked at her friends. "I thought you all would be at the festival, working or doing something. And isn't your mom in the hospital?" She looked at Daphne last.

"She is. She's being moved to Rochester today."

"And we're working at the festival, as I'm sure you are, but...we wanted to talk to you first."

That was all the time it took for Katie to realize that something was very wrong, and the light that had been in her eyes dimmed as she stepped back, holding the door open for everyone to go in ahead of her.

Chapter 20

Making time for each other no matter how busy life gets. Spend time with your spouse, show them that they are important to you. - Skye from Orange NSW Australia

KATIE LESSING STOOD back, holding the door open. She was happy to see all of her friends, but...the fact that they were all here on a school morning, especially on the day of the Apple Festival, well, she didn't want to be negative, but normally they set up a time that suited them all when they got together.

They didn't just show up at her door.

She couldn't push the ominous feeling that threatened to blacken her soul away. It just felt heavier and heavier.

"Can I get any of you some tea?" she asked, as she closed the door and followed her friends into the kitchen.

They were comfortable enough in her home that one of them went to the fridge and grabbed creamer as another pulled out chairs while a couple more went straight to the cupboard and grabbed some mugs as all of them murmured that they'd drink a little tea.

She had hot water in her tea pot on the stove.

It was old-fashioned, but she loved it because it was a bright yellow and looked cheerful and happy in the mornings. Sometimes mornings were hectic as she got her three kids ready for school, and the teapot always cheered her.

Normally Russell wasn't around, and she did most of the work getting the kids ready herself. Since he had such an important job, he needed to be at work early to set an example for everyone else. That's what he said anyway.

"Are you all going to the festival today?" she asked as she set her favorite cinnamon and apple flavored tea bags, along with green and black tea on the table.

She paused for just a moment as no one reached for it.

Her eyes swept around the table, and while Orchid seemed to be trying to push her lips up, Lavender's face was dead serious, and Daphne looked sad.

She stopped. They had been friends too long for her to continue this farce.

"There is a problem. How about you all just tell me what it is."

She stood at the table, her hand still holding the box of cinnamon tea.

Lavender and Daphne were seated at the table, and Orchid had just set mugs around.

"I think maybe you need to sit down," Orchid said softly.

Katie hated being the only one of the room who didn't know whatever it was that was making everyone look so dreary, but she sat, knowing that she felt like an underdog, so she was trying to latch on to something to get annoyed about.

Trying to school her thoughts and saying a quick prayer that God would help her be calm, she sank into a chair slowly, putting her hands on the table, folding them in front of her.

Consciously she tried to relax her muscles, but her hands wanted to cling tightly to each other, and she couldn't make herself slide back on her chair, instead sitting on the edge, her breath feeling uneven her lungs like a balloon losing air.

"I'm ready."

Lie.

But, how does one brace oneself for a terrible blow? Maybe one of them had cancer. Or maybe one of them was moving away. She didn't want to lose her friends, and she hated the idea of someone her age battling that dreaded disease.

But they could count on her support. Just as soon as she got used to the idea.

"I saw Russell in the parking lot of the C-Store about twenty miles away from Sweet Water last night."

"Yes. He had to go on a business trip. He'll be gone all week." She rolled her eyes. "I keep telling him he needs to get a job where they don't make him work so much. Often it's weekends, too."

"He's not working. He was with a woman. They kissed. It wasn't the kind of kiss that you give a co-worker."

She sat with her mouth open. Her heart stopped. The room spun, and her vision narrowed everything becoming black. Her friends disappeared. She could hear them. They were saying something. Maybe somebody was touching her hand. Maybe there was a hand on her shoulder. She wasn't sure.

Her first instinct though, was to deny.

"Are you sure it was Russell?" she asked, her words sounding like they came from far away as she lifted her head and tried to focus on Sadie's face.

"I'm sure."

Those words left no room for doubt. But, just in case, Sadie continued. "I wouldn't be sitting here today if I weren't one hundred percent absolutely sure. But, I was thinking that you can call his work. See if he's there?" She bit both lips. "I hope I'm wrong."

Katie sat there, her heart hammering, her chest hurting. Physical pain that crushed hard. Did she want to call? Of course. She needed to know. If he were safely at work, that would probably mean that he hadn't lied, that what Lavender thought she saw wasn't what she actually saw.

How did she call? She tried to bring her scattered brain together.

"I'll call." She would. Just as soon as she figured out how. When her brain started working again. Right now it felt like hardening cement and she didn't move.

"Do you have your phone?" Someone asked gently. Maybe Orchid.

That's right. Her phone. She did have her phone.

Where was it?

Her brain felt like it was struggling under water, dark and deep and unable to surface. Like it couldn't breathe, couldn't see, couldn't move, but just circled in slow motion.

She swallowed, realizing her mouth was dry, her throat tight, and she choked, coughing.

Her friends suddenly stood around her, one on one side one on the other, and one with a hand on her shoulder in the back.

She felt surrounded, but not safe. Like they were there, but she couldn't reach them, even though they were touching her.

What was she going to do? If this were true, how was she going to take care of her children? Would she confront him?

She'd have to. She couldn't live with him, knowing he was cheating on her and not saying anything.

How could he? They had three kids together.

It was true, he'd completely forgotten her birthday and their anniversary.

Funny how those facts surfaced in her brain. Did that mean he was cheating? Did she miss the hints?

"If you have the number for his work, I'll call if you want me to?" That was Lavender.

She nodded slowly. Maybe it would be better if someone else called. His secretary would recognize her number.

Somehow, she managed to dig her phone out of her pocket and put it on the table, scrolling up until she found his work number. She hadn't called him at work for a long time. He'd asked her not to call unless it was an emergency. She understood that. He got paid to work not talk to his wife. Of course. Everyone wanted their family to let them do their job unless there was an emergency.

But now she was suspicious. Did he ask for her not to call because he been doing things he didn't want her to find out about?

Funny how just one sentence, *I saw your husband kissing another woman*, could completely change her mindset. Up until that point she had been completely trusting, totally believing everything he said, with no reason to suspect that he might be lying to her, and now, she wondered if everything he'd been telling her had been a lie.

He had a big project due at work, and that's why he hadn't remembered her birthday. He was trying to land a big account and had to take a work trip and was focused on that, and that's why their anniversary had slipped his mind.

She took a deep breath, but it trembled as she blew it out. She wanted to curl up in a ball, lie under the table, get away from the pain that seemed to be crushing her. This couldn't be true. Couldn't be happening. Couldn't be her life.

"Hello, Reynolds Global Solutions, Becky speaking."

It was his secretary. She sounded the same as she always did.

"Hello Becky, I am calling to speak with Russell, please."

The words were simple. Lavender hadn't made up a fake reason to need to speak to him.

"He's on vacation and won't return until Friday. May I ask who's calling, please?"

Lavender swallowed, her throat working hard, the look on her face stricken. It made Katie feel like her friend hurt for her, a deep painful hurt, almost like the one she was feeling herself.

It was obvious that those were not the words she had wanted to hear.

Somehow the phone was clicked off, and they all sat in silence.

Katie didn't need to talk to her friends to know that what Sadie had seen was almost assuredly true. After all, if her husband was taking a vacation, surely she, as his wife, should have known about it.

Should have been with him. Their kids and her.

He told her he only had two weeks of vacation. He complained that he had to work weekends and said it should be illegal for a company to make him take business trips over the weekend. She had agreed, of course, but had never suspected that he wasn't actually taking business trips. And when he said he didn't get paid any extra for them, she believed that too.

And when he said he only had two weeks of vacation, despite the fact that he'd worked there for ten years, since they'd been married, she hadn't argued about that either. She agreed that he should have more, but also agreed that the benefits were excellent and pay good, so they wouldn't complain about the lack of vacation or the lack of overtime pay for weekend business trips.

How foolish she'd been.

"Maybe, just to double check, we should call him." Orchid spoke softly. The sadness in her voice making it sound wobbly and depressing. Her face looked just as shellshocked as Katie's felt.

No wonder. Katie would have been the last person any of them would have expected to have this happen to her.

She hadn't even thought about her family. She had six older siblings, all happily married. None of them divorced, her parents were still married, and all of their siblings had stable marriages, if not loving ones.

She wasn't the first person in her family to go to college, but she would be the first one to get divorced.

The D word. She didn't even want to think it. Had never considered it for herself, but, if Russell was truly cheating, she couldn't stay with him.

She just couldn't.

There would be no way she could trust him again. After all, she'd given him blind trust and blind loyalty and even though she still couldn't believe it, was still having trouble accepting it, she knew, beyond a shadow of a doubt, if this were true, there was no way she would want to have anything to do with him.

How could he do this to her?

"I think it would make me feel better. I'm having some really terrible thoughts. I... I don't want to destroy my marriage if what we're suspecting is not true."

"Do you think he would be more likely to pick up if you called? Or do you think he'd be more likely to pick up if a number he didn't know showed up?"

"Let me try first."

She was getting her legs back underneath her. Maybe the future wasn't exactly clicking in place, but the first thing she wanted to do was to figure out whether or not this was true.

It seemed like calling and asking would make the most sense.

She took her phone out and pressed his contact. They had children, he had a job, and she worked part-time, in order to be home when the children were, so, they didn't call or text each other much.

He was further down her list of contacts than her husband probably should be.

She pressed the green button and put it on speakerphone. Why, she didn't know, other than if she couldn't get words to come out, maybe one of her friends could.

But she didn't need to worry about that because the call went to voicemail.

One of her friends clicked off as she closed her eyes.

God? Where are you? Why is this happening to me?

She wanted it to be a dream. She wanted to wake up now. It was time for life to go back to the way it was before she found out that her husband was living a life she didn't even know about.

Vaguely she realized Lavender was dialing his number, her phone on speaker as well, sitting on the table in front of them.

"Hello?" He answered on the second ring.

"Hello, is this Russell Lessing?"

"It is. Who's calling?"

"I was hoping to speak with your wife, Katie."

"Sorry. I'm on a business trip. Katie is at home with the children. You can call her cell phone number." He hung up.

If she had wondered whether or not she would catch him in a lie, right there it was. His secretary said he was on vacation. He told a random caller he was on a business trip.

Why wasn't she crying? Why wasn't she sobbing on her friends' shoulders?

Her eyes felt dry, her throat dry as well, and she didn't feel like crying, or screaming, or doing anything. Except just sitting, curled up in a ball if necessary, and waiting until the pain turned to numbness.

What was her family going to think? She didn't want to face them, because obviously there was something wrong with her because she couldn't hold onto her husband. Because she couldn't keep him from cheating. Because she wasn't good enough.

Even though in some small part of her brain she understood that those thoughts were ridiculous, that there was a character flaw on his part where he couldn't stay true, where, maybe she hadn't been the best wife the world had ever known, but she shouldn't have to have been in order to get her husband to stay faithful.

If he had a problem with their marriage, he should have said something about it. It wasn't okay to cheat just because he wasn't happy. Although, he had not said a word about not being happy. She would have worked to fix whatever it was.

She started to fight those thoughts in her head. Then she realized, that's what her friends were there for. To tell her that this wasn't hurtful. That no matter what Russell said, she had not given him an excuse to break his vows. She had not been such a terrible wife that he couldn't stay true. And even if she had, a man who had integrity, would honor his word, would do what was right, didn't take up with another woman and then lie about it.

"Guys. I need you to help me." She laid her hands on the table, and automatically three other hands grasped hers. That was what real friendship was all about.

Chapter 21

Talk to each other. - Emy McCabe, Belmont, MA

DWIGHT FINISHED PARING an apple and sliced it in small pieces into the bowl on his lap.

That had been the thing that was the hardest to keep up with, keeping apples pared and sliced.

Two of Orchid's sisters had come into the kitchen to help. They, along with Miss Charlene and Miss Kathy had made sure that the apples had gotten measured, seasoned with the spices, and that the dough had gotten made and rolled out.

The ovens had been going nonstop since they started, and still they were hard-pressed to stay ahead of the crowd, who seem to be buying apple turnovers at an alarming rate.

Dwight wasn't super concerned about any of that though. And he didn't mind being the only man in the kitchen, either. While cooking would probably never be his thing, and paring apples wasn't his favorite job, he didn't mind. It was for a good cause, and it was fun to be a part of something people love so much.

Still, his heart was heavy, because he heard the whispers, and knew where Orchid was.

One of her friends had discovered that one of her friend's husbands had been cheating on her.

He knew better than to question God's timing, but it was hard not to.

She was just starting to trust me, Lord. Our relationship was moving forward, and now this.

She had already had trouble thinking he would stay true. If one of her friend's husbands had been caught cheating, that would bring all those doubts and fears to the surface, and, he was afraid she would look at him and see all the things he had in common with that husband.

Not that he even knew the man.

Maybe he was just blowing things out of proportion, but he felt like Orchid had been working through those fears, but now they would be back in her face.

He pared another apple, letting the waste fall into the bucket at his feet.

Maybe the problem with this type of work was there was too much time to think. He needed to have faith in Orchid and what they had been building together.

She knew what kind of man he was, and that's what she had been falling in love with. His character and integrity. She said as much. Maybe she hadn't used the word love, but he felt like that's what they were working toward. A strong relationship built on shared values, on the character of both of them and the idea that they would live with integrity and respect for each other.

The buzz of voices in the kitchen shifted, and he lifted his eyes.

Orchid stepped in. The other ladies' hands stilled as they looked at her. But her eyes went to him. His hands stopped, too.

He couldn't keep himself from setting the pan aside as he rose, his eyes never leaving hers.

She looked crushed, dejected. Like she'd been crying, even.

He threw his knife and the apple he'd been working on in the pan as he walked toward her, his mouth suddenly dry. His heart hammering.

To his relief, she met him halfway, her arms wrapping around him as he enfolded her and pulled her close.

As he lay his cheek on her head, his eyes met Miss Charlene's. She gestured toward the back room where they'd been storing the apples and extra flour and sugar.

He'd been back there several times carrying things to the kitchen, and he jerked his head at Charlene. She was right. That would be the perfect place for him to take Orchid to talk.

"Let me wash my hands and we'll go to the back room."

She nodded her head against his chest but didn't move.

He didn't want to leave her, but he didn't want to stay here in the kitchen with all the eyes on them, when he had so much in his heart that he needed to say.

Or maybe, even more that he needed to hear.

He didn't bother with soap, just washed his hands so they wouldn't be sticky, barely dried them, and took Orchid's hand, sliding it against his, clasping it with his fingers, wishing that sealing their hearts together was that easy.

She'd been in conversation with Rose, and he didn't pull her away.

But she said, "Talk to you later," and moved to go with him.

Rose gave an understanding smile at Dwight, and he felt like he had her blessing.

Funny how that eased his heart more than anything she could say would have.

If Orchid's family approved of him, that would go a long way toward easing Orchid's mind as well. She respected and appreciated her sisters, brother and mom. They made up the foundation of her world, and he knew their opinion would be essential to fulfilling his desire to have a relationship with her.

They walked in the room. He turned around and shut the door, the lights flicking on as he hit the switch at the same time.

He wanted to turn and pull her back into his arms, but if she needed to talk, he didn't want to take that from her, or overshadow that with his need to touch her, feel that she was real, that she was still with him, that nothing had changed, even though he thought most likely, everything had.

"You heard?"

"About Katie?"

She nodded.

"Yes."

"I've never wanted to murder someone so badly in my life before. Just take a skillet and beat him to death with it."

There was so much anger in her words they shook.

He understood, at least in theory. The idea of wanting to hurt someone who hurt someone he loved.

He would want to do that to anyone who hurt Orchid.

"I guess I don't really want to do that, but I'll go with you." He wasn't sure where those words came from, but he realized as he said them that they were the truth. He wanted to be with her no matter what she was doing. Not that he wanted to kill someone, and maybe, he would be with her just to try to talk her out of it, but he would still be there. Beside her. Through whatever happened. Because he cared.

His words made her head jerk up, her eyes wide. "I think you really would."

"I would. Might try to talk you out of actually killing anyone, but I'd be there."

She nodded, slowly, like she was thinking about that along with everything else that had happened to her.

"I was sorry to hear that about Katie." He wanted to insult her husband, belittle him, say what a slimeball he thought he was, but he didn't want to come off as sanctimonious either. He'd done his share of stupid things. Even immoral things, or things that showed what a lack of character he had. And, by insulting someone else, he didn't make himself look better.

"It was devastating. None of us wanted to tell her, someone had to. The jerk's been getting away with it for far too long. It wasn't hard to talk to a few people who knew what was going on."

"What she is going to do?"

"I'm not sure. She didn't want to do anything off-the-cuff. Even though the guy's a jerk, slimeball, sneak, Katie wants to handle it the way a Christian should."

Orchid pulled her lip back. "I think I was angrier than she was when we left. But she called her mom, and she had her sisters helping her with the kids when they get home, and she was going to pray about what she should do."

"Wow. I don't know that I would be that calm."

"Me, either, but I think it really helped to have three of us there, beside her, telling her it wasn't her fault, and encouraging her to do the right thing, as much as I wanted to grab a hold of his throat and just smack his head against the wall."

"I didn't realize you were so violent."

"I didn't either." Her eyes were sincere, and she sounded half aghast at herself for even thinking such a thing.

"She's not kicking him out?"

"I don't know. She had said she would, and then she said it wouldn't be right for her to be unkind just because he had. But I don't think there's any hope of reconciliation. Jesus gives one contingency for divorce, and that's fornication. So, divorce is perfectly acceptable, and I would think it would be the preferred way, although there are people who have been able to forgive."

"Seems to me, that unless God works in his life in some kind of supernatural way, if a man's a cheater, he always will be."

"That's what I was thinking." Her eyes lifted to his, and the lead weight of dread sucked his stomach in. "A man who has character, who is someone you can depend on, is hard to find."

He didn't say anything, because she seemed to be saying more with her expression then she was with her words.

"I thought about Russell, her husband, and, I'm sorry to say, I compared him to you."

He wanted to close his eyes, hang his head back and howl. He could almost hear her next words, saying that she thought they were exactly alike, or something along those lines. Like being a celebrity baseball player automatically made a man lack character. Even though he knew that to not be true.

"I thought about how you spent the last eighteen months trying to talk to me. Trying to get me to notice you. Asking me out, being turned down, and not giving up." She looked down at the crate of apples sitting at their feet. "Russell had never cared that much about Katie. He was very easy-going. He never seemed protective or devoted. I know that can get out of hand, where a man doesn't want to let his wife out of his sight, wants her to ask permission before she goes anywhere or does anything. Wants to control her. So not what I'm talking about. He just... Didn't seem to care." She lifted her shoulders. "I don't how else to explain it."

He waited. She didn't seem to be saying what he had been afraid she was going to say.

But it seemed a little premature to hope. Although, an optimist by nature, he had to hope. The lead didn't feel quite so heavy in his stomach.

"He didn't pursue her." Her words were thoughtful. "It almost felt that one woman would do just as well as any other. Maybe he lacked loyalty."

She lifted her eyes.

"The exact opposite of you. You came here, you wanted me, and you didn't quit. You pursued me. Even when I said no. You weren't a jerk about it, and you weren't creepy, but you let me know you wanted me, and you waited. You waited until I was ready. You didn't give up and go to someone else and someone else and someone else. You stuck."

He couldn't let that pass. "That's because you're special. There is no one else in the entire world like you." Maybe saying in the entire world was a bit of hyperbole, but he meant it. Maybe. "If there is anyone else, I don't want to know them. I only want you."

For the first time that day, her lips curved up. Even though there was still heavy sadness in her eyes, his words had touched her the right way. He wasn't usually very good at saying the exact right words, but he was pretty sure he had just now.

"I think love is a risk at any time. A relationship, commitment. You never know when the other person will keep their word or not. If we didn't have a problem, we wouldn't need arbitration. There wouldn't be divorce. People would just do what they said. So, there is a risk, but I feel like if you would wait a year and half for me to just say yes to you asking me out, that says a lot."

"You're worth waiting for. You're worth giving up whatever it takes to have. There isn't anyone who comes close to being what you are to me."

She shook her head. "I don't even understand how you can look at me and see something that is so much different or better or more worthy than anyone else, but that's a gift."

He held his breath.

"It's a gift that I want to cherish. I... I want to be with you."

Her words were soft, said in a bit of a rush, and breathy like she was scared. But she plunged on. "Not just because you seem to think I'm somehow amazing and special, but because you are too. You're funny and kind, and how many men would sit in a kitchen full of ladies paring apples just so they could be with me? Would work in a sale barn, cleaning manure off cement, particularly when your real job pays so much. That really impressed me. Not that you liked me so much, but that you had that kind of character."

She met his eyes directly, and the weight in his stomach was completely gone. His heart smiled, and it was almost like in the distance he could hear the beginning strains of the Hallelujah Chorus.

"I was afraid when I started hearing what was happening this morning, that Katie's husband had done what he did, I was afraid you would have the exact opposite reaction. But somewhere in my heart, I believed that you had seen me for what I am, and not through the tarnished lens of what other men might do."

"When I look at you, I see honor and integrity. I see loyalty. I see humor and someone who wants me to laugh and enjoy life with him. I see someone who's not going to leave me. I see someone who isn't afraid to work to be better. To admit that he's not perfect and wants to grow. I see a man who wants me to be happy, and he treats me better than I ever dreamed someone would."

"I want to point out that I'm still practicing. I might even get better."

"Maybe I'll get better too."

"Does that mean we'll grow together?" He stepped forward, tugging her to him. She came willingly, taking both her hands and threading them around his neck.

"I hope so because life is a lot more fun when I'm with you. Whether it's making apple turnovers, which I'm looking forward to, or working in the sale barn, going wherever you want me to go. It wouldn't be fun without you. But with you, I can't wait."

Her words warmed him from the very bottoms of his feet, clear up to the base of his head, radiating joy out. He felt like there should be rainbows and unicorns dancing around.

"It might be a little dangerous for me to kiss you when you're talking like that, but it's what I want to do."

"I'm pretty sure we'll be okay. We're in the church, with pretty much all the ladies in the entire town standing outside this door."

"I have a feeling I might not care."

"That would make two of us. But I wouldn't want to ruin your good reputation."

He snorted at that and lowered his head, pressing his lips to hers, and everything that he thought would happen, did.

He forgot his name. Forgot where they were, forgot how to stand, forgot everything but her touch and her taste and her scent and the feel of her, soft and warm, under his hands.

He pulled away. "I love you."

His words were slow and distinct and as heartfelt as he could make them.

He'd never said them to anyone before, and he didn't want them to sound like he was just shooting them off, meaningless and empty, because that was what a man said when he kissed someone. Because it wasn't. It wasn't something he'd said just because he felt he should or it was expected. It was something he said, meaning he was making a commitment, a pledge, a life event where she meant more to him than anything else in the world, and he would give up whatever comforts he needed, whatever was necessary in order to show his love for her.

She pulled her head back just a little, searching his eyes, as though she could read from his tone that the words came from the very depth of his soul.

"I love you, too. And I want to spend the rest of my life showing you how much."

Those were the words that were in his heart, the ones that didn't come out of his mouth, but were there in his tone. She'd caught them exactly, giving voice to them, and handed them back to him, laying them at his feet.

"That's how I feel, too." Those words were simple, but every bit as heartfelt as he could make them.

He found, that while she might need the words at some point, she understood the emotion now.

Their lips met again, and it was a while before they went back out to help the ladies finish the apple turnovers.

Epilogue

"I heard that Dwight Eckenrode not only proposed to Orchid, but he put an offer down on that old rundown farm just north of town, the one that's been on the market for more than a year, but no one wants to touch because it needed so much work."

All the Piece Makers sat around the table, teacups in front of them. They had been working on a quilt and had just finished up that morning and were all taking a break now. Soup simmered on the stove in the back, and Charlene should really get up and stir it, but she'd been thinking.

"I heard that too. I also heard he had a highfalutin architect in to look at it, and, instead of bulldozing the house, they're going to fix it."

"I heard about the highfalutin architect, but I also heard that he had a local fella taking a look at it as well. And he hadn't decided whether he was going to go with the big city firm or give the North Dakota fella a chance."

"He's hiring the North Dakota guy," Charlene said with reassurance. She'd just talked to Dwight last night. It had been a month since the Apple Festival, and he told her that Orchid had said yes, and had shown her the ring.

He thanked her for her advice, and then asked if he could ask her something.

She hadn't been expecting what he said.

He thought he knew who the father of Daphne's daughter, Powell, was, and he'd asked Charlene if that was accurate.

Charlene had been floored.

She'd never considered it, but, in her mind's eye she saw Powell, and she saw the man Dwight had suggested. She didn't see how he couldn't be right.

She hadn't figured out though, whether Daphne knew. Could she really know who the father was, live in the same town with him, and not tell him that he had a daughter?

And the man. He lived in Sweet Water. But he didn't treat Powell any differently than any other kid that lived in town.

Could he really not know?

And, if they truly didn't know...how did that happen?

"I don't think they're going to have a big wedding. They can afford it, but neither of them want to do anything fancy. I think they're just going to get married in the church and have a lunch afterwards."

"In the next couple of weeks if I heard correctly."

"There shouldn't be rules when it comes to weddings. You should do what you can afford, and what you want, not what society dictates." Charlene believed that with all her heart. Weddings become a royal headache, with so much stress and expense.

People stressed more over their weddings than they did over their marriages. They spent more time planning their weddings than they did on trying to keep their marriage together.

Sometimes the wedding wasn't even paid for before they had to pay for a divorce.

She didn't think that would be true with Dwight and Orchid. She'd never seen a couple who wanted to be together more than they did. It was hard to catch one of them without the other anymore.

She hoped those feelings lasted. It was sweet to see. Sweet to see two people who lived the Bible definition of love. Where each of them were more concerned about the happiness of the other, and were willing to sacrifice whatever it took.

Two people who were completely devoted to each other, who were loyal.

Dwight got the credit for that, since he started it.

And Orchid...what a blessing to have a man like that.

Charlene allowed herself to think about that for a little bit longer, because it warmed her heart and soul to see that kind of devotion, before the analytical part of her mind insisted that she go back and try to figure out what in the world she was going to do about Daphne.

THANKS SO MUCH FOR reading! If you'd like to read the next book in the Coming Home to North Dakota series, *Cowboy Looking at Me*, you can get it HERE[1].

Listen to the unabridged audio performed by Jay Dyess HERE[2] on the Say with Jay channel on YouTube. Hear many of Jessie's other books performed by Jay for FREE on Say with Jay.

I'd love for you to sign up for my newsletter[3] to read about my daily life on the farm, be the first to know about my new releases, get deals on my books and occasionally get other sweet romance deals as well.

---

1. https://www.amazon.com/gp/product/B0BF5ZJJP6
2. https://www.youtube.com/c/SaywithJay/videos
3. https://dl.bookfunnel.com/oox4p9mesw

Made in United States
North Haven, CT
08 June 2024